LUCKY

Also by Henry Chang

Chinatown Beat
Year of the Dog
Red Jade
Death Money

LUCKY

HENRY CHANG

SOHO
CRIME

For Lucas

* * *

Published by
Soho Press, Inc.
853 Broadway
New York, NY 10003

This is a work of fiction. Names, characters, places, and incidents
either are the products of the author's imagination or are used
fictitiously. Any resemblance to actual persons, living or dead, to events,
locales, or organizations is entirely coincidental.

Library of Congress Cataloging-in-Publication Data
Chang, Henry
Lucky / Henry Chang

ISBN 978-1-61695-784-1
eISBN 978-1-61695-785-8
1. Yu, Jack (Fictitious character)—Fiction. 2. New York
(N.Y.) Police Department—Fiction. 3. Chinese—United States—Fiction.
4. Chinatown (New York, N.Y.)—Fiction. I. Title.
PS3603.H35728 L83 2017 813'.6—dc23 2016044300

Printed in the United States of America

10 9 8 7 6 5 4 3 2 1

JACK

Honor

IT WAS A sunny morning, the second Monday in April, and NYPD detective Jack Yu quickened his pace, stepping briskly toward Confucius Towers with a takeout bag of *sooksik* food tins, a pack of illegal RedRockit firecrackers from Lee Bao's grocery, and a flask of whiskey.

He also had a Colt revolver on his hip.

From late March through early April, with winter still hanging on, Chinatown barbecue shops were swamped from *hoy dong* opening until midafternoon, lines of the dutiful trailing out the door down along the sidewalk, folks pressing impatiently for the *char siew* and *for yook* and *see yow gai*. The triumvirate of Cantonese *sooksik* for Ch'ing Ming observances—roast pork, soy sauce chicken, barbecued spareribs *leung tew gwut* were the essential fast-food elements for a visit to the Chinese boneyard.

Ch'ing Ming is the Chinese memorial period when friends and relatives grave-sweep around headstones and burn death money, cash for expenses in the beyond. People were now said to be burning bigger denominations of death money since inflation hit the afterlife. *What,* Jack mused, *the paper Louis Vuitton handbags and the cardboard Mercedes cars weren't enough?*

Because they believe that underworld windows are temporarily open on the *other* side, families celebrate the spiritual connection and share the *sooksik* snacks like a communal picnic, spread out around the grave area. In rainy weather they eat standing under umbrellas, drinking from vacuum cartons of soy milk or chrysanthemum tea, sharing desserts like *bok tong go, wong tong go, dao foo fa*.

They pour *bok jo* wine into the earth, light candles and incense, and plant bouquets of flowers. Flower shops and Buddhist stores thrive during the Ch'ing Ming period.

Easter around the corner, Jack thought, and meanwhile a lot of *real* money being spent on death money and condos for the dead.

The two main cemeteries for the New York City Chinese were in Brooklyn: Evergreen Hills and Cypress Valley. Many of the old-timers bought plots there when they realized they were never going back to China, but there were lots of Chinese in Queens now, farther from Chinatown, where they'd bought up large sections of the Maple Grove and Flushing cemeteries.

Pa was buried at Evergreen and it'd been almost three months since Jack had last visited, in the dead of winter on Pa's birthday in January. That was the second time he'd gone alone, without Alexandra, whose grandfather was also buried at Evergreen.

Alex had big problems of her own, a messy yuppie divorce that threatened to involve him. He remembered how it felt with her naked next to him. For a moment, he lost himself in the thought of it.

* * *

HE'D MEANT TO visit the cemetery earlier, but a complicated Chinatown case had swallowed a couple of weekends, and the mental health day he'd earned now came in handy. On the second Monday in April, he was already very late, toward the end of Ch'ing Ming.

Billy Bow's Mustang made the going easier, and this late in the season on a weekday, he hadn't had to wait for the takeout.

His Chinatown friend Billy Bow had embarked on a one-month sex tour of Thailand, to all the usual places—Bangkok, Patpong, Chiang Mai—and had generously loaned Jack his black 1986 Mustang GT, a nine-year-old souped-up and chromed gangsta ride with tinted windows.

The Mustang had been Billy's main ride before he got married, *cruisin' his pimp an' pussy mobile* he'd called it, and after the ugly divorce, it reminded him how it felt to be free. He'd loaned it to Jack under the condition that Jack left a full tank and returned it to its monthly parking spot at Confucius Towers.

Billy didn't want the car left on the streets overnight.

The Mustang was an automatic. It had a moonroof, power windows and locks, and a bumped-up stereo he'd gotten from Canal Street. It was powered by a five-liter V-8 engine, and Billy had bartered for the mag wheels and chrome hubs, tinting the windows himself at Charlie Chang's chop shop on Pike and South. *Charlie took cash only, no receipt.*

The car looked prime for a gangsta drive-by. The NYPD and DOT had outlawed the blacked-out windows, and cops harassed boom-box cars for noise violations, hoping for a bigger bust for weed or alcohol. It wasn't the kind of car you'd expect an Asian NYPD detective to step out of, unless he was undercover.

The incense and death money Jack needed were already in the black car's trunk, along with an empty five-gallon soya-oil tin can from the Tofu King. Billy had cut the metal top off to allow for the burning of the death money and to contain the exploding firecrackers. He'd also included a plastic container of *bok tong go*, gelatinous sweets from the Tofu King. *For that lawyer chick of yours*, he'd teased.

Jack crossed the Bowery to the high-rise building and took the stairs down to the garage.

The Paki attendant brought the Mustang up from the bowels of Confucius Towers Parking and got tipped a dollar. There were several attendants and Billy had explained to them about lending his car to his friend.

Billy had told them that Jack was a badass cop, and they always brought him the Mustang quickly and deferentially.

The car growled like it needed to swallow some asphalt, and before Jack knew it, he was roaring down the expressway.

Driving the Mustang, Jack could get to Evergreen Hills in just twenty minutes. Traffic was light—it was mostly heading in the opposite direction, into Manhattan—and he switched up the radio from a rock station to some easy listening. He rolled his shoulders as the Mustang practically drove itself.

The appointment with the NYPD therapist wasn't for another two hours, plenty of time to get to her office in lower Manhattan.

The mellow music shifted his thoughts to Alex, *Alexandra Lee-Chow*, a passionate Chinatown lawyer with whom he'd become intimately involved. Fleeting images of their nights together were crowded out by subsequent legal complications.

Trouble was, her scummy soon-to-be-ex-husband had gotten his hands on a security videotape from Confucius Towers, a tape that captured him and Alex in the elevator going to and from her apartment in the Chinatown highrise. *Proof of their movements in the wee hours.*

The tape would position Alex as an unfaithful wife, and because Jack was a tainted cop, would also show her as an unfit mother. Attendant lawsuits perforated the already acrimonious divorce proceedings, and Alex had broken off contact with Jack to protect her seven-year-old daughter. They'd last met at a Lower East Side sushi bar. *Temporarily*, she'd promised him, changing her cell-phone number, declaring that they couldn't be seen in public afterward.

He understood, knew she was protecting the custody case. But that was three weeks ago. And he missed her.

He turned off the radio as he arrived at the cemetery. It was peaceful. There weren't many visitors this late into the Ch'ing Ming cycle.

He followed a serpentine road until he came to a knoll at the Chinese section along the edges of the cemetery. There was sparse green in the stands of trees and the earth was brown-gray and barren. He'd planted a pair of Dusty Millers, bookending Pa's headstone. He wondered how they'd survived the winter.

He parked the car, got his supplies, and headed toward the deserted knoll with its crooked lines of headstone tablets.

He could almost hear Pa's complaint.

Come so late. Why come at all?

He put down the bucket and bag. The branches of the Dusty Millers had withered somewhat but showed tiny buds of new life. He plucked away a few dead leaves. There would be yellow flowers in the coming weeks.

He ran his hand briefly over the headstone, over Pa's Chinese name carved into the rock, before gathering up branches that had fallen near the grave.

He kicked away twigs and pebbles and other winter debris, and when the site was clean he took the *sooksik* tins out and placed them on top of the plastic takeout bag.

He took out his metal flask and poured a circle of XO into the earth at the base of the headstone.

"*Chaai lo ah?*" he heard Pa's derisive words. "Too busy arresting your own people?" That conversation wasn't what he'd come for, and he took a swig himself before pocketing the flask. Three months hadn't erased much of the guilt he still felt.

If anything needed to be swept clean, it wasn't the

grave site. It was the grief in his heart from not having had the chance to say goodbye, make amends *son to father*.

The son, the cop. Always after the fact.

He fired up the incense. Now wasn't the time for apologies. He'd offered plenty at the funeral, the Thirty Days After visit, Pa's birthday in January.

But when he presented the incense, he thought, *Yeah, Pa, sorry I'm late. Yes, they've got me arresting my own people, but only the bad ones.*

He took a breath. *And I never take money.*

He took the first bow imagining his father's eyes on him. *Today I remember and honor you.*

He bowed again.

Today I sweep away all the dead things.

He bowed lower for the third time and held it longer.

Today I burn death money to ease your way.

He planted the three sticks of incense at the head of the plot and readied the tin bucket at the foot of the grave. He flamed his lighter to the packs of death money and dropped some into the bucket. He fanned out the bigger denominations and fed the flames until the billions in death money was consumed.

After the fire died out, he placed the *sooksik* on top of the headstone, the way Pa had taught him. *The dead are in the ground. Do you feed their heads or their feet?*

Feed your head, Pa, he heard himself thinking.

He uncovered the tins and nibbled at the *cha siew* and the soy sauce chicken, imagining Pa having his fill of everything. Later, he'd pack the leftovers and take them home.

The grounds were barren, but the way the sun washed across the soft hills felt nurturing, ready for rebirth. He took another hard swig from the flask and lit up a cigarette. Poured the last of the whiskey into the ground.

Almost an hour had gone by and he took a final look at the skeletal branches of the Dusty Millers. Imagining them in full yellow bloom, he wondered if Pa would have approved. He packed up the leftover *sooksik* and stepped back to the foot of the grave.

He took the pack of firecrackers from his pocket and put the tip of his cigarette to the fuse. Dropping it into the bucket, he offered a last bow.

Today I chase away the evil.

The explosions thundered inside the tin bucket and his ears pinged the same way they did on Chinese New Year, always a time of new beginnings.

He deposited the blackened bucket, with all the burned remains, into the cemetery's refuse bin.

ON THE WAY back, he left the radio off and thought about the NYPD shrink session scheduled for the afternoon. The therapist's name was May McCann, and she had an office on Duane Street in Tribeca. Walking distance to Chinatown.

The session would last an hour. He wondered what kind of questions she'd ask.

Brooklyn neighborhoods flashed by as he considered what to discuss with her. After all, the session would be a matter of record, and could reflect badly on his law enforcement career if he said the wrong things or created the wrong impression.

He knew she'd ask about the shootings, the main mental health focus for the NYPD. Questions would branch out from each time he pulled the trigger of his Colt Special. Meanwhile, he'd finally decided to switch over to the Glock 19, a semiautomatic pistol that could chamber a nine-millimeter bullet with fourteen rounds backup.

She'd probably ask about the dozen dead bodies that had made their way across his desk. He felt okay with that, with the ones *he* hadn't killed. *Lowlifes killed each other, that was their problem. Not his.*

She'd definitely ask about the two men he killed in Seattle, two Chinese triad thugs intent on stopping him from saving a woman of interest.

She'd also want to ask him about having been wounded. *Both flesh wounds, including one just inches from his heart.* He'd want to downplay them. He decided he didn't really want to talk about dreams, or nightmares. It'd taken him a long time to put his nightmares behind him, especially the Ying gang's fatal stabbing of his boyhood friend Wing Lee, a dozen years earlier. He'd boxed bad dreams into a corner where they rarely bothered him.

Of course he'd had dreams of intimate moments with Alexandra, but he felt the need to keep her out of the conversation, especially since he could become embroiled in her divorce case. And he didn't want to discuss strippers at Booty's, including Soomi the Korean bombshell import.

But he was willing to talk about certain nightmares that he could downplay to his advantage:

—A snarling pit bull lunging out of the dark at him. The black gangbanger swinging a baseball bat at him.

—The Chinese thug with the big knife, coming out of nowhere. Another triad hitter approaching for a kill shot as he desperately tried to reload the Colt.

—The Chinese *see gay* driver trying to stomp him off the Pell Street rooftop.

He was reliving all those moments as he found a spot on Duane and parked the Mustang.

Duty

FORTY-FOUR DUANE STREET was a no-doorman high-rise building with an intercom and buzzer system. Jack knuckled No. 2, and after a moment a woman's voice answered.

"Dr. McCann's office."

"I have an appointment."

"Your name?"

"Jack Yu."

"You're a little early, detective. It's the second door on the right. Please make yourself comfortable for the time being."

She buzzed him in and he went through the second door to a windowless room paneled in blond wood. There was an austere couch and chair setup, everything tan or taupe. *Professional*, with no personal touches. A Parsons table in one corner supporting a jade plant in a terra-cotta pot. A matching table in the opposite corner with a bamboo tray of bottled water.

The faint scent of sandalwood made him wonder if there was a *feng shui* setup involved.

No other adornments to the room. No wall art or psych magazines or Muzak.

He shed his jacket and took a seat on the couch. He remembered to take the Colt off his hip and placed it into his jacket pocket. *Am I facing northeast?* he wondered. Taking a meditation breath, he scanned the walls. There were no visible door handles, meaning each wall panel could be a door.

He wondered where, and when, she'd make her entrance.

After a minute, he imagined the lights dimming just a touch. *Showtime,* he thought.

A door opened in the center of the wall opposite him, and a woman stepped into the room, a pretty Asian face framed by long black hair. She wore a dark blue skirt suit over a light blue blouse, and black business pumps with barely a heel. *Tall for Chinese,* he thought, certain she wasn't Korean or Japanese.

"I'm Dr. McCann," she said, locking the front door. She was anything but the older white woman he'd expected. *McCann? Maybe it's her married name?*

"Jack Yu," he answered, noticing there was no wedding band on her ring finger. *Maybe divorced but hung on to the name?*

"Thanks for showing up today, detective," she said with a smile.

"Wouldn't miss it," he replied coolly. She looked early twenties, which for an Asian woman probably made her late twenties. *Maybe she was an adopted child?*

"We'd been canceled once before," she reminded him.

"Yes, I got caught up on a case."

"It's okay, I understand completely." She sat in the

chair opposite him and crossed her legs modestly. It wasn't as if she'd worn a miniskirt, her style conservative and professional, but her legs were long and toned like a runner's. *Tanned, like she'd been in the sun.*

He found the sight of her exhilarating yet distracting. He'd intended to get the session over quickly but now didn't know where to begin. She wore her suit jacket open, and he could tell the blouse was tailored, form-fitted.

"I've read your file, detective. Let's get started, shall we?"

My file, he repeated to himself. *My jacket.* She'd opened his jacket and had searched his soul. *Of course she knows everything that happened.*

"So you want to talk about the shootings?" he asked.

"Detective," she said earnestly, "I do appreciate your cooperation. But if you let *me* ask the questions, we'll get through the session quicker."

"Sure." *Be conciliatory. Agreeable.* He leaned back on the couch, returned her smile.

Body language, he was thinking when she leaned forward, her blouse pushing against the suit jacket.

"Let's start with the most recent shooting. On the rooftop in Chinatown?"

The smile came off his face. "I chased a murder suspect up to the roof. He pulled a knife and I got cut."

"You discharged your weapon how many times?"

"Two. Maybe three."

"You didn't actually shoot him?"

"No." He looked into the short distance between them, licked his lips, knowing he shouldn't have.

"Why not?" she pressed.

"He dropped the knife."

"Would you have shot him if he hadn't?"

"Yes, if he came at me."

"But he didn't?"

"No. He made the right choice. I had the drop on him."

"What did you say to him?"

"I brought up his ancestors."

"His ancestors?"

"How he could meet them real quick." He fought back a grin that came out like a smirk.

"You challenged him?"

"I wanted any reason, any move."

"To kill him?"

"To shoot him, yes. To take him down." The frown returned to his face.

"You didn't want to kill him?"

"I wanted to arrest him, but I knew I was bleeding out. And I wasn't going to let him escape."

"You were ready to shoot him?"

"If necessary. I needed to cuff him."

"What defines 'necessary'?"

"Any move toward or away from me. He wasn't getting away."

"No escape?"

"It's happened before."

"In San Francisco?"

"That's an open case, too." He was impressed. She'd taken a good look inside his jacket. "A perp got away."

"How do you feel about that?"

"I don't like people getting away with murder."

"You desire justice?"

"You could say that."

She got up from the chair and went to the Parsons table. She handed him a bottle of water before sitting her long legs back down.

"Thank you." He took a big swig before she continued.

"What happened in the Smith Projects?"

He flashed back to the ghetto housing projects, *jing foo low*, just outside of Chinatown.

"It was just a black kid with a .22 popgun. I was lucky. He wasn't."

She crossed her arms and waited for him to continue.

"I wounded a perp. Killed a dog." *Downplaying it all the way.*

"You should have been scheduled *then*," she said. "How did it go down?"

"It happened like *that*." He snapped his fingers. "All I saw was jaws, flying at me. I shot. Just reacting. There was a guy swinging a bat. I shot two, three times." He paused. "The dog crashed into me. A table fell over. I kept shooting."

She stared at him and waited.

"Then everything was quiet. Until the EMS came. Other cops too."

"How did you feel?"

"I was afraid, like my life could end right there. But they had it coming. I had to defend myself. Just trying to stay alive." She nodded, moving him along.

"The department justified the shooting. By the book," he said.

She made some notations, shifted her body, crossed her legs the other way. Brushed her hair back with her hand. She leveled a look at him.

"Okay, let's move on to Seattle."

He remembered the big Chinese thug who came out of nowhere, barreling into him. He saw in his mind the second hitter approaching, aiming for a head shot.

"You shot and killed two men?"

He remembered his canned response.

"They were trying to kill *me*. I was defending myself."

"You're good at self-defense?"

"So far I've been lucky."

"Do you count on being lucky?"

The question made him think of Chinatown gang leader and boyhood blood brother "Lucky" Louie, lying in a coma at Downtown Hospital.

"No," he answered. "Odds are your luck runs out at some point."

"How do you feel about killing them?"

"Look, they attacked me and I killed them."

"It's that simple?"

"I don't take it to bed with me." He thought his answer threw her off beat momentarily.

"What happened in that case?"

"That case is still open. Can't say much except that I apprehended an unrelated perp. And there's still a missing woman."

"Okay, we can come back to that. You've been wounded two times, correct?" Her rat-a-tat style made him hesitate.

She'd excluded the *shuriken* attack in Seattle, the sap to the head on Pell Street, and the bone-deep slice to his elbow. *But maybe those hadn't made it into his jacket yet?*

"*More*, actually . . ."

"I mean *gunshot* wounds?"

"Well, yeah, then you're right. It's twice."

"Tell me about your first wound, your left arm."

He took a *shaolin* breath through his nose, found his balance on the couch, and leaned forward. "During the course of an investigation I encountered a person of interest. We had a fight and he pulled a gun and I got wounded. A graze wound in my left bicep."

"What happened to the POI?"

"Is that relevant?"

She gave him a look that reminded him who was in control.

"He got killed later, not by me."

"How do you feel about that?" She rested her hand under her chin.

"Nothing." He shifted back on the couch. "He was a bad guy, got killed by another bad guy."

"Okay, your second wound?"

He remembered a fleeting image, someone running and firing shots back at him. "That was the black kid in the Smith Houses." He dry swallowed. "I was lucky again."

"What happened in that case?"

"They killed a deliveryman. I hope they do a long

stretch." He took another sip of the water as they paused, letting the tension subside.

"Have you had nightmares, detective?"

"Not really. Nothing job related."

"And the men you killed?"

"Just part of the job."

"Is there anyone you can confide in? Parents? Siblings? Someone you can spill to?"

"No one."

"No spouse? No girlfriend?" She rested her hand on her chin again, assessing him.

"No girlfriend." He shook his head, keeping Alexandra out of it. "No spouse." He thought he saw a tiny smile cross her face.

"And no dreams?" she asked again.

"No, no dreams." He didn't want to talk about the nightmares. They'd make him look like damaged goods, and he didn't want *nightmares* slipping into his personnel file. And now he wondered if she was coming on to him, in some subliminal way, because she'd made him nervous the same way that Alexandra did when they first met.

"So no bad feelings, no nightmares? Everything is okay?"

"I'm okay," he lied again, thinking she's heard all this before, like cops reading from a cue card. *What did she expect from cops anyway? Right, I get nightmares all the time. I had to turn to self-medication. I don't see the public the same way anymore. I'm the last in my family line, and I'm alone. No relationship to speak of. I'm depressed. I'm damaged. I'm fucked up. I need psychiatric help. What cop is going to confess that?*

Instead everything was just *line of duty*, *nothing personal*, *didn't bother me in the least*.

"You know it's unhealthy to keep things bottled up inside?" That look again from her.

"There's nothing bottled up," he said.

"Nothing personal, just line of duty?" She narrowed her eyes at him.

"Exactly."

"That's what ninety-nine percent of officers involved in shootings say."

"Well, must be the truth then." He smiled.

"So you're *disaffected* emotionally?"

He was cautious about the terminology making him appear dysfunctional somehow, and was unsure how to respond. "I just didn't take any of it personally. Just moving on," he offered.

"Moving on?"

"Just to get back on the job."

"Aren't you on the job now?"

"But I'm being checked out, my mental fitness."

"It's just due diligence on the part of the department. You know it's for your own good?"

"Yes, you've been a great help."

"You're not patronizing me, are you?" she asked through her smile.

"Patronizing? I wouldn't disrespect you that way."

"Okay, excuse me. I'll just be a minute." She got up abruptly and disappeared behind the wall-panel door. He thought he heard her rustle some papers.

He finished the bottle of water, wondering how much time was left in the session. He felt he'd been there forever.

She reappeared, and instead of sitting down she unlocked the front door.

"We're done for now, detective. But we need to schedule a follow-up." Surprised, he got up from the couch.

"Again?" Now he was the one asking questions.

"We need to discuss . . ."

"What?"

"The man on the rooftop, for one."

"The immigration cops iced him. Kicked him back to China. That's it."

"Okay, but the department requires a follow-up. I'll have an outline for the next session."

"When?"

"I'll contact you," she answered. "There's no rush." She opened the front door, held it for him. Still in control.

"Okay, thanks for your help," he said without feeling, catching a glimpse of her pretty face as the door closed. He was already pushing out the front exit when he heard her office door locking behind him.

Crossing the street, he couldn't help feeling wrung out, on the wrong end of a pysch wrestling match. Then lashed by a velvet whip.

The cold afternoon revived him. He shrugged his shoulders, rolled his neck. He couldn't remember the last time he'd splurged on a full-body massage.

Shrinks, he mused, *gotta be wound tighter than white on rice.*

Desire

THE MUSTANG WELCOMED him like a warm glove, and he drove it east, toward *Fook-Jo Land*, his nickname for that northeastern edge of Chinatown populated mostly by Fukienese Chinese, the latest wave of immigrants from South China.

As he cruised East Broadway with the window down, the wind felt good on his face, blowing out the bits of images and emotions that May McCann left adrift, like bullet fragments, in his brain.

He saw where the neighborhood blended over—Hasidic, Latino, black, Chinese—cultures clinging to times long past. *We were supposed to move on, through the generations, and assimilate into good Americans. Whatever that is.*

He took a loop through the Lower East Side, *Loisaida*, past the welfare projects all in a line along the East River—the Smith, Wagner, Rutgers, Baruch, and Gouverneur Houses—patches of black and Latino and stranded poor whites, from South Street to the East Village.

The loop brought the Mustang back toward Chrystie Slip, where the AJA had its community storefront, and where he knew Alexandra would be. AJA was the Asian American Justice Advocacy, a grassroots community organization providing outreach to victims of domestic abuse, violence against women, and sex trafficking, as well as to immigrants falling through the net of NYC social services. It got its juice from pro bono lawyers and local activists. *Chinatown.* Not just in Manhattan, but in Flushing, Queens, as well. Chinese grandmothers arrested for selling *joong* wraps and *bok gwor* shelled beans on the sidewalk. Chinese truckers harassed and ticketed by DOT. Complaints from shop owners and restaurants about unfair scrutiny of Chinatown businesses. *The city should be glad for the tourist revenue.*

They're fucking the golden goose, Billy'd said.

The thought reminded him of the vulgar emails Alex had gotten her hands on, copied, and shown to him in her fury and alcoholic despair. The scumbag side of her husband she'd never seen before.

He remembered a few of the emails in their brazen glory.

Brianna Johnson: "*Luv oral. My mouth on ur cock.*"

Frank Chow: "*Sucking me.*"

B: "*U came in my mouth.*"

F: "*U swallowed.*"

B: *"Luv the taste of U."*

F: *"I came 3 times."*

B: *"I lost count, how many 4 me . . ."*

F: *"Luv ur Ass."*

B: *"Luv Anal."*

F: *"backdoor brianna, haha."*

B: *"Doggie do-right, hah."*

F: *"Hitter in the Shitter, hah . . ."*

The graphic content stunned them. And now he'd become part of the problem.

STOPPED AT A red light, Jack hoped the sugary gelatins would sweeten Alex's day.

He turned onto Chrystie Slip and spotted an open space in front of the storefront, near the big black-on-yellow AJA banner. The Mustang slipped into the space easily, giving him a front-row seat behind the car's blacked-out windows. He could watch the entire storefront, *like on a surveillance setup, observing without being seen.*

He killed the engine and waited.

Through the big windows he could see Alex's office door was closed. There was a receptionist working a desk out front, and he was wary of the security camera covering the main door and the desk. Alex didn't depend on the camera protecting her, he knew, because she packed a .38-caliber Ladysmith and knew how to use it. He knew because he'd taught her.

He picked over the leftover *cha siew* and the soy sauce chicken he'd brought back from the cemetery. Since they were in the lunch-hour swing, he hoped to catch a break, hoped the receptionist was a late-luncher.

As he munched the last piece of *see yow gai*, Alex's door swung open. She carried a stack of envelopes to the receptionist, who put on her coat. *Hitting the post office before lunch?*

He watched her exit with the stack of envelopes, making a right toward the local post office on Houston.

He saw Alex manning the reception area and casting a wary glance his way, at the old-school gangster ride with the black windows parked right outside. She seemed preoccupied, a lone lady honcho in an empty storefront.

When the receptionist turned the corner Jack grabbed the container of *bok tong go* and slipped out of the Mustang. He saw Alex suddenly jerk her attention in the direction of her office. *Great*, he thought, a chance to surprise her with the sweets.

He entered quietly after Alex retreated to her office. She was on the phone and he couldn't help but overhear. Her angry words froze him at the receptionist's desk.

"You want the FourRunner that badly, Frank? I *saw* your emails. *Blowjob* in the backseat? *Really*, Frank? The two of you fucking in the FourRunner, huh? You want the car? YOU CAN HAVE IT! But you think I'm going to let my daughter ride in that car ever again? Screw you, Frank. Screw you and miss 'Backdoor Blondie.' I'll see you in court, you lowlife piece of shit!"

She slammed the phone down, hyperventilating, as upset as he'd seen her that day a year ago, when one of the female uniforms brought her into the Fifth Precinct on a possible D&D, *drunk and disorderly*. He'd saved her from possibly being disbarred, putting his own reputation at risk. "*Baggage*," Billy'd warned. "That lady comes with *baggage*."

Enraged, Alex stormed out of her office, then was startled seeing Jack at the desk. She caught her breath.

"How long have you been standing there?" She was fighting back tears.

"A couple of minutes," he said quietly.

"That son of a bitch. We have a court date in two weeks and he's trying to drive me crazy. Sorry you had to hear all that." She saw the container from the Tofu King in his hand. "That for me?"

He handed it over, bringing a small smile to her face. He wanted to hug her, hold her close and comfort her. Glancing up at the security camera, he held back. A security camera had been the cause of their troubles.

"You could come out to Brooklyn," he offered, "if you need a break." She'd never been to his apartment in

Sunset Park, where they could have some privacy, maybe even some intimacy. "No one knows us out there," he added.

She moved closer to him in a way that partially shielded her from the security camera. She put a hand on his chest, over his heart. "I miss you too, Jack. But we need to cool it, like we agreed."

"I understand. Just trying to help."

"I know. And I've got Kimberly all week. Off school holidays." He had no answer for that.

"But it's good to see your face, hear your voice," he heard himself saying.

"Can I get a rain check?"

He smiled, remembering all the "rain checks" she'd given him before he accepted the cup of homemade espresso that led from her kitchen into her bedroom at Confucius Towers.

"I miss you too," she repeated in a hush. "I hope you know that." She ran her hand across his chest again before leaning back. "Thanks for the *bok tong go*, but you better get going before Victoria gets back."

They glanced out the front window at the empty street.

"She's picking up our takeout lunch." He was glad to see she'd calmed down a bit.

"Okay, I'm out," he said, taking her hand, giving it a soft squeeze. *Awkward, but sweet.* "But don't worry, I'll be in touch," he promised, backing out under the security camera and through the street door.

Alex was smiling at him even as he got into the black muscle car parked out front. He threw a quick smile over his shoulder in her direction before disappearing behind the black glass windows.

Billy's sweets would take the bitter taste off her tongue, he thought as he pulled away from the curb.

Will the court allow the videotape from Confucius? she wondered, watching the Mustang pull away. She looked at the container of *bok tong go* and retreated to her office. Though the anger still twisted her heart, at least Jack's desserts would sweeten the bitter taste in her mouth.

THE ROLLER-COASTER EMOTIONS of the day kept him off balance but had worked up his appetite. His brain was numb but his stomach growled. The afternoon had gotten cold and dark in a hurry and he decided to return the Mustang to the garage. He could hop a *see gay* radio car back to Sunset Park.

He imagined a big bowl of hand-pulled noodles, beef *lai meen,* and a side of spicy tofu at one of the Fukienese soup shacks on Eighth Avenue. *A round of cold beers from the fridge couldn't hurt either,* he thought, urging the Mustang home through the waking neon colors of the Bowery.

Scars

STEAM FILLED THE small bathroom, but he could still see his naked reflection in the mirror. A boxer's body, *wiry, taut, muscled.* The Fuk snack shack had left him thirsty, and he was looking forward to hitting the six-pack of beer in the fridge and whatever was left of the bottle of XO.

In the mirror, he traced his scars, fully healed now but looking raw in the fluorescent bathroom light.

From the top down, an angled three-inch scar on his left bicep, like the hash mark uniformed officers wear on their sleeves, signifying years on the force. *Courtesy of the tong enforcer Golo's bullet.* Below that, two small oval scars on the left side of his chest, slightly above the heart, where a gangbanger's little .22-caliber bullet had passed through. The mirror fogged up, but he could still see the puncture scars on his left forearm, these being more jagged, from the clamp of a pit bull's teeth.

The hot shower brought his blood to the surface, made his skin tingle and his throat clutch. He wasn't due to report until the next afternoon, covering the four-to-midnight tour of Manhattan South. A long night's rest awaited him.

He grabbed a beer mug and a sake cup, took two icy cans of Heineken from the fridge, and brought everything to a folding table. The bottle of XO there had at least two shots remaining, he guessed, cracking a can and pouring it into the mug. He filled the little sake cup with a shot of XO and dropped it into the foaming beer. *Boilermaker*, he mused, *Asian style*.

He remembered how they drank when he was in Army Airborne. Chugging the mug, he fished out the sake cup, poured another shot of whiskey, and cracked open the second can of beer. There was still one shot left in the bottle.

He sat on the corner of his bed, powered up the TV, and took a gulp.

On the TV, Springsteen the boss man singing "Streets of Philadelphia."

He channel surfed through a mix of programs:

—Massacres and genocide in Bosnia. Serbs and Croats in a toxic mix.

—The AIDS epidemic and "Streets of Philadelphia."

—The aftermath of a nerve gas attack in the Tokyo subway system. A Japanese cult blamed for eight deaths.

—An old-school performance by WAR, *what is it good for?*

The United States "rescuing" Mexico with a $20 billion aid program.

He muted the sound, let the images flow by like a slide show. Another gulp of beer turned his thoughts around to Alex, as dystopian images flashed across the screen.

He knew there was no future in memories, and *the lady got baggage*, whispered the bitter divorcé wisdom of Billy Bow. Was he really going to fall between mother and daughter in a custody fight? *Ready to be a stepfather to a young child who would probably despise him?*

Still, he hadn't felt this way about anyone in a long time, and Alex had stirred his desire. *Desire,* that wise woman Ah Por warned, *was the root of all suffering.*

He took another swallow of the boilermaker, felt the alcohol seeping into his brain. He took two slow settling breaths, keeping his balance as more disconnected images chased across the godlike screen.

He drained the rest of the mug and let his eyes close momentarily, oddly picturing Pa's tombstone and May McCann's legs. His thoughts slowly fragmenting, he got another beer, switched off the room lights, and mixed the last boilermaker by the kinetic glow of the TV.

The room went black when he turned off the screen. His eyes adjusted to night light from the street outside, slipping in along the edges of the window blinds. Sitting up in bed, he let his thoughts drift and took another swallow.

He was hoping to get to oblivion and back without dreams, or nightmares, along the way. He took three deep *shaolin* breaths. Buddhist chants filled his brain, *nom mor nom mor nom or may tor fut*, and he let himself go.

LUCKY

Damn Lucky

YEAH, IT WAS *like a dream*, he realized later, *like a crazy long-ass dream. A bang and a sudden burning flash of white light. Then he was gone, how long he didn't know.*

He could hear the doctors talking among themselves. He heard comments from visitors, hospital workers, but was unable to respond. Unable to open his eyes or speak. Unable to move a muscle. Then there was the medicine, which made him punchy in the beginning.

Words from the doctors he didn't understand. *Encephalon. Pons Varolii. Ganglia, cerebellum.* More pieces he couldn't put together. *Motor cortex, fibrillae. Optic thalamus.*

He learned he'd been shot. *Two to the head, surprised he wasn't dead.* IV medication escorted him in and out of the darkness, but sometimes the orderlies and nurses who attended to him left the wall television on while they worked. *Not like they were disturbing him, right?*

He heard snippets of news, time and dates. *February became March.* He started regaining feeling in his fingers and toes, knees and elbows.

"He's lost twenty-five pounds," one of the male nurses said.

"Well, he was a chubby Chinky when he got here," the other said, laughing.

His clothes were nearby, he knew. The orderlies conspired to steal the eight hundred in cash in his Gucci wallet. Planned to take his Oyster Rolex, and his 18K gold braid chain and medallion too.

"This gangsta got some fine shit, yo."

"Quiet! He'll hear you."

"Hahaha. He won't need any of dis where he's goan."

He understood thievery and hijacking, so the prospect didn't faze him, didn't trouble him as much as what he'd heard from other visitors, speaking freely because they'd been told he lay in a coma. They assumed he wasn't *hearing* anything.

He recognized their voices. Pai Kwut's was nasally, and Yeen Jai's was like gravel tumbling in a can. Two of his Mott Street crew, street names Spareribs and Cigarette Boy, already writing him off, figuring how to split his shares.

He pictured them—Spareribs, tall and skinny, and Cigarette, built like a fire hydrant, always with a cigarette dangling from his lips.

Payback will be a bitch when I come home, he thought.

"We're taking over his Las Vegas nights shares, and the Kino from Baxter Way." A dry cough from Cigarette.

"I'm getting the sports book at Eddie's," declared Spareribs. "But Hammer wants the numbers out of Mon Lai Wah."

"What about the weed?" That raspy voice. "The ecstasy?"

"Taiwan and Loy Sung got their eyes on that." *Two outside dailos whom he never trusted. Taiwan and his crew from Flushing. Loy Sung and his Bronx Boyz. Now he knew for sure.*

"Think he'll wake up?"

"Hope not." They laughed as they left the ICU.

Cocksuckers. See what happens when I get back.

Another time it was Charley Joe, *Big Uncle Jo*, a gang handler from the On Yee Association, with his phlegmy, watery voice. He pictured him through his eyelids— *overweight, a comb-over on his Buddha head—bossing people around.*

He was with Dup Choy, a 426-rank enforcer for the Wo faction within the On Yee Merchants Association. Nick-named *Hammer. A burly six-footer, more flab than muscle, spoke like he had a mouthful of marbles. Mumbles Choy.*

"We're paying the bills here." Charley Joe's wet voice. "He'll be released into our care once he wakes up."

"*If* he wakes up. Den wat?"

"Then the *kai dai* motherfucker better have all the right answers."

Shit they wouldn't dare say on Mott Street, to his face, without getting a kneecapping, at least.

"We'll take him out to Long Island."

Not if I can help it, fuckers.

"We need to get that pad back."

The notebook he'd taken from the safe at On Yee headquarters. *Leverage*, he understood. *Names, dates, pay-offs. Murder for hire.*

"What about his crew?"

"They don't care who's boss as long as they get paid."

"All about the money."

"The dogs are grateful, for now. Not for long if they sniff out how much we're really holding back."

"What else?"

"The Hakka powder."

Chasing the dragon. Smokable Number 3.

"Two kilos."

"We got Chow's construction crew, took apart their crashpad. *Nothing.*"

Did they really think I was going to hide it in the clubhouse?

"So we need to find out."

Too late. Already sold to Tony Biondo, ha. Powder to cash, suckas.

The IV meds dragged him down again. *Motherfuckers . . .*

Somewhere along the way, the voice of Jacky boy, blood brother now hated Chinatown cop.

"This how it ends for you?" from the sentimental sap. "Another wasted life?"

Please.

The doctors came and went.

"Could be synapses connecting again."

"But he hasn't shown any movement?"

"No."

He kept still whenever he heard anyone in the room. Voices from the TV told him March had become April. *April Fools' Day.*

He was able to open his eyes again, and could make out

shapes, movement in the darkness. Almost blinded when daylight arrived, he sneaked periodic glances until his eyes readjusted.

Soon after, during the night shift, he was able to lift his legs and bend his arms. Humming quietly to himself at first, he found his voice again. *Did they think they were going to get rid of him that easily?*

"Payback," he whispered, "is gonna be a *motherfucker*."

Rude Awakening

A CHAIN OF images rattled his boilermaker oblivion, like grainy videotape unreeling in his forehead. A New Jack City crime blotter. *Someone in a ski mask robbing a Chinese laundromat. A Taiwanese clerk pistol-whipped in a liquor store. On the Lower East Side, a Cambodian girl raped in a Thai massage parlor. A Korean woman escapes by fighting back.*

A robo-alarm going off somewhere. *Louder.*

Jack jerked up in the darkness, staring down the numbers on the clock radio. It was 4:44 A.M., cursed Chinese numbers. The alarm was his phone jangling, an urgent bleat to it. Nobody ever called in the dead of night, and at first he hoped it might be Alexandra bearing good wishes, but on Easter Sunday morning, he dreaded it could only be bad news.

He held back as the machine cue went to voice mail. A beat, then an edgy female voice.

"Hello, Detective Yu?" *It wasn't Alexandra.*

He knuckled off the recording, picked up the handset.

"This is Detective Yu." He took a slow gulp of air.

"This is Downtown Hospital. We're calling as you requested."

He rolled his neck. *I requested?*

"Your friend has recovered. He's being discharged."

"My friend?" His head still fuzzy from the alcohol.

"Yes, your friend Mr. Louie?"

Louie? Tat "Lucky" Louie? He rubbed his temples.

"Detective Yu?"

"Yes."

"He asked that you come right away."

"Why?" he asked as she hung up. He got out of bed, reaching for his clothes and his gun go bag.

It was like his dark nightmare coming true. On a black Easter Sunday morning, ex-Chinatown blood brother Lucky had risen from the dead.

Rush

THE SKY STILL inky at 5 A.M. He caught a *see gay* on Eighth Avenue, rushed the night driver to Confucius Towers. The blur of highway lights brought back the case files in his head. Tat "Lucky" had gotten shot during a shootout outside the Chinatown OTB on the thirteenth of January. *Friday the thirteenth.* He fell into a coma a few days later, lasting until April 16, *Easter Sunday.* Eighty-eight days dead.

Arisen on Easter Sunday. The number eighty-eight was a double-helix double-lucky Chinese number. Religion and superstition all leaning his way. He was lucky, after all.

The sleepy Paki attendant at Confucius Parking brought the Mustang up quick, conditioned by the tip mode. From there it was a three-minute shot to Downtown, the car at his disposal. Not to depend on a cab or *see gay* if the scene went sour. He could use his cop parking privileges with impunity.

He powered the windows down. The cold wind and the adrenaline drove the alcohol out and cleared his brain as he sliced south past Park Row, taking the back streets to Downtown Emergency.

ICU/I See You

HE BADGED PAST the nurses and staff, saw a group of Chinese around Lucky's bed. Three of them. One guy, short and balding, in a suit. Another one, looked like the muscle. The third guy looked light on his feet, had his eyes on everyone. Slightly built, not a fighter, so he was probably armed. A planner. An *officeholder*.

The head of hospital security was a beefy red-faced Irishman, retired cop from the look of it. He motioned for Jack to come his way, at a distance from the three Chinese men around Lucky.

"What have you got?" Jack asked. The man seemed impressed, or relieved, by Jack's New Yawk English.

"Those men are his caretakers of record," McMahon said. "They've been yapping in Chinese, about what I don't know. Got a little heated. Mr. Louie refused to go, insisted we call you."

Mr. Louie. Jack wasn't used to Lucky being tagged so formally, like conferring priesthood on the worst sinner. "What's next?" he pressed.

"Well, they've signed off on the paperwork."

Jack clipped his badge near his gun, patted it. "Yeah, but *this* trumps *that*."

"You're arresting him?"

"He's a person of interest. I'm taking him for questioning."

McMahon grinned and gave a cop-to-cop nod.

"Well, the lad's all yours then."

Lucky, fully dressed, waved to them from the bed. "Mr. Officer!" The first words he'd heard from Lucky in months.

"Mr. Officer!" Wearing a sneer disguised as a grin. The coma apparently hadn't deleted the wiseass part of Lucky's brain.

The fathead with the bad hair glared at Jack but the tall muscle kept his mouth shut. The lightweight, *officeholder*, spoke for them all.

"We have his discharge papers."

Jack flapped open his jacket, flashed his gold shield and gun. "And I got his discharge right here."

Everyone was silent a moment, frozen by Jack's words.

"Yeeaah, cowboy!" said Lucky, laughing. "See, you don't wanna mess with Officer, I mean, *Detective* Yu."

"Shut the hell up, Tat," Jack snapped.

"This man is our client. We're responsible for his care." Lightweight, trying to step up. "We demand he be released to us."

"These motherfuckers trying to kidnap and torture me!" Lucky swore. "I go with them, you never see me again."

That could be a good thing, Jack thought. The orderly who'd dressed Lucky brought a wheelchair.

"He's been released to my custody," Jack said. "You can

get him at the precinct when I'm done with him." He never said *which* precinct.

Lucky stared down the hospital orderly. "Jamal, enjoy the eight hundred cash you and Tyree took out of my wallet, *bro*." He looked from Security Chief McMahon back to Jamal and grinned. "And my Rolex, if you haven't fenced it yet, is worth $10K. Don't hock it for peanuts. Know what I'm sayin', *homeboy?*" Saying it *street* just the way he'd heard it numerous times with them hovering over his inert body.

All eyes locked on Jamal, who frowned, offering "Here's ya wheelchair." He excused himself and quick-stepped from the ward.

McMahon helped Lucky into the wheelchair.

The comb-over muttered, "*Dew nei lo mouh,*" mother-fucker.

"Suck my dick, Charley," Lucky said, sneering.

Tall muscle said, "You're a dead man."

"Just *finished* being a dead man, Choy," Lucky said. "What? You gonna kill me twice?"

McMahon escorted Jack as he wheeled Lucky away, with the gang of three following at a sullen distance. They went down the ramp to the curb where the Mustang was parked.

"Whoa," Lucky exclaimed. "You brought the *pimpmobile?*" Jack helped him slide into the backseat as McMahon watched.

The three *caretakers* piled into a black sedan parked a block away. The dead of night obscured the details.

"Just like the old days, huh?" Lucky said. Jack ignored him, fired up the Mustang's headlights.

"I can get you Witness Protection if you give me something to work with."

"Still need to be the hero, Jacky boy?"

"And you still got that death wish, Tat?"

"Ha, I get another chance to die twice."

"They're not going to stop until they get you. You know that."

"I'm not planning to hide."

"I *could* take you in for questioning."

"Stop frontin', bro. You got nothing. And if I drop dead in your custody, how's that gonna look?"

"There's that death wish again."

"*Fuck* dat. Stop preaching and drive." *Useless to argue with a dead man*, Jack thought, *and besides, he was right.* There was nothing to hold him on that the gang's white-shoe lawyers wouldn't slice and dice. Along with a formal misconduct complaint to the department.

Jack pulled away, watching the dark Chevy Impala in his rearview. It was banging a U-turn into traffic to get on his tail. Lucky lounged across the backseat, grinning.

"Give me your phone," he demanded.

"Where are we going?" The Impala in the side-view now, four cars back.

"Just like old times," he repeated, looking out the back window, welcoming the challenge. "Go right on Park Row." The tail jockeying in the rearview again.

"Straight to East Broadway. Give me the phone." Jack

tossed it to him, gritting his teeth as the Mustang bit into the blacktop. He knew these backstreets by memory, having done this before in their younger years. Back then it was *joyriding*.

Lucky punched in a number, waited. "Meet me on the street," he said. "Five minutes."

Toward the end of East Broadway, Jack didn't see the Impala anymore.

"Left on Grand!" Lucky ordered, returning the phone. Jack could tell Lucky was just holding on for the ride, having come out of a coma into a car chase. He gunned it, braking left before spotting the dark car again, farther back but still in the slow chase.

"Hard left on Delancey."

He skidded onto Grand and braced through the slam left, then twisted west three blocks until the split fork into Broome. The Mustang would be out of sight by then, and when the tail got to the fork, they'd have to stop, make a decision. The short streets they'd face led in three directions and a dead end.

They'd never pick up the Mustang after that.

Jack doubled back past Chrystie Street, where a tall woman wearing a floppy hat and a black down coat was waiting for Lucky. He struggled out of the car and turned to Jack.

"Better roll, Jacky boy. They might still be cruising for us." He scanned the street. "I'll be in touch, bro."

The woman helped Lucky, rubbery-legged, toward a building in the middle of the block. There was no sign of the Impala as Jack slowly pulled away, watching them in the rearview. *188 Chrystie.* He vaguely remembered the location; he knew there was a whorehouse on the street, run by a woman named Angelina Chao. Billy was a regular, and had offered to treat him to some pussy, but even in his loneliness, he'd declined.

He wondered if it was Angelina who Lucky called, if the number tapped into his cell phone belonged to her.

He planned to return later. In his condition, Lucky wasn't going anywhere far. *188 Chrystie? And who was the woman?*

He took a right on Hester, crossing back through Chinatown. Daylight had broken, and he decided to grab something to eat before reporting to the Ninth Precinct. Halfway through a plate of *yeen gnow faahn* at Half-Ass, his cell phone sang.

"Detective Yu?" It was Dispatch. "Your twenty?"

"I'm in Chinatown," he replied. "Copy?"

"Report to the Fifth Precinct."

"Come back?"

"See Captain Marino."

Before he could ask any questions, she'd hung up.

THE FIFTH PRECINCT was the oldest in the city. Stylized numbers *1881* scrolled across the top of the Chinatown building. The creaky steps and groaning floorboards led the way to Captain Marino's office. He stood at his desk, and the look he threw at Jack's arrival was not a happy one.

Inside, Jack saw two familiar faces, Detectives Hogan and DiMizzio, Internal Affairs cops who never passed up a chance to make his life miserable. In the past, they'd laid a minefield of allegations, allegations from wealthy Chinatown Chinese that were full of innuendo but always short on proof. They'd succeeded in thwarting his investigations nevertheless.

He wasn't happy that the department always seemed to take the side that was against him.

It struck him that he'd known bulls like Hogan and DiMizzio all his life, racist cops who taunted Chinese victims and perps alike with their special brand of Chinglish. *Wottsee motta? No speakee Englee? Confucius say no tickee no washee? Hey China doll likee sum yung gai? Hahaha.* *Gwai lo* faces, howling white devils in blue uniforms, occupying the foreign port, Chinatown, where everything was one pungent *chingchong* Chinese fire drill.

Don't worry about it, Jake, it's Chinatown.

Jack wasn't surprised that Pa had hated cops. Hated them more since his only son also became a *chaai lo*, another dull brick in the blue wall. "*Tong yen* come here long time," Pa would complain, "but Melica no good to Chinese. Make go away. Chinese work hard, but make go away." He'd heard it a thousand times, Jack thought, and it was what drove him into the army, into the NYPD, the America of the father not the America of the son.

Captain Marino gave them the nod, and Hogan with the crew cut led off.

"You hijacked a known criminal from a hospital bed."

"Yeah, your old pal, Tat Louie," bent-nosed DiMizzio chiming in.

"A Ghost Legion *dailo*."

That didn't take long, thought Jack. The Tong's Chinese handlers at the hospital siccing IA on him.

"A *POI* at the OTB shootout. And you helped your homeboy escape."

They waited to see how Jack took the bait.

In his mind, he no longer let their taunts bother him, tucking them into the *fuck you* file in his forehead.

"You finished?" he responded. "First thing, if we had something to charge him with, we would've done it in January, when the shootout happened. Second, those men at Downtown, *your* pals, were planning to torture and kill him."

"You coulda brought him in. Sit 'im and squeeze 'im."

"On what grounds?" Jack challenged.

"Make something up."

"So his fancy lawyer can accuse me of harassment again? Been there done that."

"It ain't a popularity contest."

"*Bullshit.* That's easy for you to say."

"*Oooh.* Combative attitude."

"Goes against the stereotype, huh?"

"You could have questioned him."

"I did. In the car."

"Where is he now?"

"I dropped him off at Chrystie and Broome." No lie there.

"And then?"

"I drove away."

"That's it? So he's in the wind?"

"He said he'd contact me."

"He said he'd call?"

"His exact words: 'You'll hear from me.'"

"And you'll take a lie detector . . . ?"

"Like hell I will. But nice try anyway."

"We'll be watching you, Yu."

"You should try watching *criminals*. Like the ones paying you to chop-block me."

"Fuck you."

"Fuck you likewise."

"Shut up alla yus!" Captain Marino growled. "Is this fucking high school or what?" He turned his wrath on Hogan and DiMizzio. "You two get the fuck out of my office." He pushed them out, slammed the door behind them. Turning back to Jack, he warned, "I don't care if he's your goddamn *homeboy*, you better keep him outta my fucking precinct, got me?" His bearish girth, and the weight of the brass on his shoulders, leaning on Jack.

"Gotcha, Captain," Jack heard himself saying as he headed for the door. "I'm *on* it."

He could feel Marino's eyes scorching his back.

HE PARKED THE Mustang a block away, on the other side of Chrystie Park. It was well into the morning rush, and the junkie slugs of the Lower East Side were nowhere to be seen. *Lining up for their methadone fixes*, Jack figured.

He could see things better now in the daylight. What had once been a tenement was now a renovated condo building. The main entrance was a gated metal door on Chrystie, but at the back side of the building on Broome Street there was a door leading to a tiny elevator. It could fit four people at most and required a key start for the fourth and fifth floors.

He went back to the main door and waited. He planned to offer Lucky safe haven if he agreed to Witness Protection and relocation.

After fifteen minutes, a tenant exited the building, and seeing Jack was Chinese, never gave him a second glance. He slipped inside and went up the stairs. It was clean and quiet up to the fourth floor, but he could hear music playing softly from the floor above. *A Hong Kong love ballad.*

There were two doors on the fifth-floor landing, both painted red. He went toward the one where the music was seeping out.

He rapped on the door. There was no answer, but he thought he heard a rustling sound from inside. He rapped again, waited. A soft metallic click from the peephole on the door, and then the music died down.

He knuckled the door a third time, took out his badge, and held it up to the peephole. There was another long pause and the rattle of a door chain being set. Then the door opened a crack and a female voice said, "*Ah Sir? Yauh mouh gaau chor ah?* There must be a mistake."

He could only see half her face, with the top of her head wrapped in a towel like she'd just finished a shower.

"We already paid off this month," she continued, her eyeball scanning him up and down.

"I'm not prostitution police," Jack replied. *Pussy cops would be how Billy Bow would have put it.*

"I'll call the lawyer then."

"You do that and I'll shut you down. I just want to talk."

"Talk? About what?"

"A man came here last night."

"That's nothing new. And how do I know you're a real cop?"

He slipped his detective's card through the crack.

"You can call the precinct if you like."

She closed the door and he imagined her making the call. Or not. He waited a few more minutes before the chain rattled again and she let him in.

The condo spread was a two-bedroom converted to three, with a pass-through kitchenette in the corner. A lineup of barstools there and metal folding trays. *A seat and a treat?* he wondered. Everything was soft tones, pastels, probably flattering in dim light. He followed her to a small seating area with a couch and coffee table. *Nothing illicit or slutty so far.*

In the empty quiet of the place, he imagined a room full of hookers and johns, alcohol and music and after-hours pillow talk.

Now the curtains were pulled back, and he refocused on the lady, or *mommy*, in front of him. He hadn't gotten a good look at her when he'd dropped Lucky off.

The streetlights were dim and she'd worn a floppy hat, but she was tall enough. Dressed only in a flimsy bathrobe, she looked late forties, and even without makeup, he could tell she had a natural beauty.

She gestured toward a chair and took a seat away from him, keeping a glass coffee table between them. On the end table beside her sat a tangerine and a large kitchen knife. *Close at hand.* He didn't think the knife was for the tangerine, and knew the *mommy* was an old pro.

"I dropped my friend off last night," he began. "You came out and helped him inside."

"*Ah Sir*, you can see there's no one here but me." She waved her hand at the bathroom, her closets. "You can look around if you like."

Being cooperative now, Jack thought, *hoping he'd be quick, then leave. A quick john.* He checked the rooms. There was no sign of Lucky, not even under the bed.

"So where is he?" Jack said.

"I have no idea who . . ."

"Look, lady, you think I'm playing? *Nei wan ngo ah?*" Slang, the way they talked in Hong Kong movies.

She shrugged her sturdy shoulders, shook her head.

Jack took out his cell phone, tapped the redial of Lucky's night call from the Mustang. He waited a moment until a phone jangled in her robe pocket. He could see flashing lights through the thin fabric there.

"Are you going to answer that?" Jack asked, watching her face as her phone danced and sang in her pocket. The look in her eyes said she knew she'd been busted. She took the phone out, forced a look at the digits, and brought it to her mouth.

"Hello," she said reluctantly.

"Well, *hello* . . ." Jack replied sardonically.

There was an icy pause until Jack continued. "You keep playing around and I'll shut you down. Put a cop on your door." She twisted her lips into a frown.

"I didn't come here for trouble," he added. "Like I said, I'm not *sex* police." *A mean cut, but just right.*

She caved and slid the phone across the glass top of the coffee table to Jack.

"Two calls," she offered. "One to Fai Ma. The other, I don't know." She lit up a cigarette as he studied the numbers, copied them into his own cell. She watched him the way an alley cat watches a stray dog. *A running dog.*

When he was done, she added, "A car came for him. Don't know where they went."

"This was daylight?"

"Yes."

"Who was in the car?"

"I couldn't see." Jack narrowed his eyes at her.

"The car was black and had dark windows." She snuffed the cigarette.

"Time?"

"Had to be around six-thirty."

Jack put away his cell as she stood up.

"I don't know anything else, detective. Now, if you don't mind, I'd like to dry my hair."

"Sure," he said. "But if you think of anything . . ." He

pointed at the detective's card she'd left on the coffee table.

"Of course," she answered, "*Ah Sir*."

Happy to see him leave.

BACK IN THE Mustang, he tapped up the unknown number and the call went straight to a beep prompt. A *pager*. He hung up, made another call. The manager at the phone division happily offered to provide Jack the unlisted pager details if he came up with a subpoena.

He hung up.

Fai Ma, or "fast horse," was a *see gay* car service on East Broadway at the edge of Chinatown, a short drive. The storefront was small, a tiny office. Two chairs, a desk, a set of phones, and a computer screen. A no-nonsense Chinese lady dispatcher. *Probably had a big room in the back where the drivers could relax and take the edge off the end of their shifts. Alcohol and gambling, bootleg cigarettes from the Fukienese crime groups.*

The lady had a cardboard cup of *nai cha* steaming on the desk, and glancing at Jack's gold badge, quickly decided legal matters were above her pay rank.

"*Maatsi ah, Ah Sir?*" she asked. "What's up?" Though she clearly didn't want any part of it.

"I need a destination."

"Trip?" She pouted.

"Around six-thirty. From Chrystie Street."

She took a sip of the *nai cha* as she fingered through the binder of trip sheets.

"Here, Chut Jai's car. Went to 14000 Thirty-Ninth Avenue."

"Flushing?"

"*Mo chor*. You got the answers, Ah Sir. No need to arrest me?"

"*Fong gwo nei*," he said, smiling. *I'll let it pass this time*.

"You know I'm here," she said coolly, pursing her lips and blowing steam off the tea.

He had to chuckle, stepping back out to the cold of East Broadway. The Mustang could get him to Flushing in twenty minutes, going in the opposite direction from the traffic crawling into Manhattan.

Pulling away from the curb he wondered how long a *see gay* pro would take to get to the other Chinatown.

HE GOT TO 14000 Thirty-Ninth Avenue in twenty-six minutes. No rush, the car just taking what the highway allowed, but Main Street was a drag. The place had a sign that announced IMPERIAL GARDEN, but there was nothing imperial about it, and it was nowhere near a garden. The Chinese takeout joint had been shuttered, its metal roll gates down and locked. There was scorching, traces of a fire on the metal.

This wasn't Lucky's true destination, Jack figured, but was the area he'd wanted. *Never give your address*, Lucky had advised, wise even then as their teenage Chinatown lives had spiraled away from them. *Let them track you down. At least they'll know who you were*.

He knew who Lucky was, understood what he'd

become, a *dailo* street boss, running a Chinatown crew of twenty-four Ghost Legion gangbangers. *Not a lucky number, twenty-four,* Jack thought, *but that's how the numbers rolled.* The end result was like *foo gwa,* bitter produce.

He believed he could get Lucky relocated, save his life. *Witness Protection?*

He needed to check the local precinct for any Chinese gang or criminal activity in the area.

At the moment, though, all he had were two dead ends.

LL Lucky

Cumback baby

THE LADIES LOVED Lucky.

The whores were the ones who saved him, the whores he'd plied and gifted with knockoff designer handbags, bootleg wristwatches and fistfuls of ecstasy and dirty money. Hos who'd sucked the life from him now giving it back.

They'd taken him to a hooker hostel to recover. A converted single-family home in New Hyde Park, just across the Queens line into Nassau County, Long Island. Where pimps housed their trafficked whores during their two-week swing through New York.

The location wasn't accidental. The pimp crew knew the communication between city cops and island cops was substandard, due to the different organizational commands. NYC cops often didn't know about island cases and vice versa.

Staying under the radar was *sing mook*, pragmatic. This secluded patch of New Hyde Park seemed like a good place to hide.

A *van jai* brought the hookers into and out of Queens

for the day or night tours in Flushing. The *Dai Huen Jai*, Taiwanese Big Circle crime group, ran a hot-sheet hotel and massage operation on a hill overlooking Main Street where it crossed the expressway.

Hookers "R" Us. 24/7. *Sick* pussy money.

THE WHORES SHARED their reinvigorating soups and ethnic comfort food with Lucky, their teas and potions nursing him back.

Thai cutie Bettie Bootwang boiled up a lusty *tofu laksa* that nourished him for two days. She made him *hock gee ma* for dessert.

Ah Won *jeer* was local Toishanese, also a monthly regular at Angelina's. A pretty face cooking up *pei daan jook* congee with an OD of *yeen say* cilantro. She brewed him *Teet Gwoon Yum* tea, liquid strength from the Goddess of Mercy.

Marisol Flores, *china-dominicana*, a firecracker body serving up an extra mean *sopa de mondongo*, had also massaged him. *Everywhere*.

Feeling had returned to his feet—legs, calves, thighs— energy coursing everywhere through his body, including his *lun* cock. The hos took care of that as well, Lucky's generous *dailo* rep preceding him.

Before he knew it, three days had passed and he was back to old tricks. Alcohol and sinsemilla. *Thank you, Bettie and Marisol*.

These ladies he loved worked for *gai wong* Jojo Yang, pimp and small-time drug dealer. Lucky knew Jojo had had a beef with the On Yee when Charley Joe's faction muscled him out of a massage-parlor deal. Jojo was Chiu Chao, tough-minded, which meant he held a grudge. In addition, Lucky had always treated Jojo's ladies well, and Jojo appreciated that.

The Chiu Chaos were a main line to Southeast Asian heroin, but Jojo was only a small-time dealer. His priority was pussy. And money.

It wasn't by chance Lucky had paged Jojo Yang. *After all, who knows better how to treat a man than a posse of whores?*

And Jojo had waited on Main Street as agreed. Riding shotgun was Jadine Jung, his *bottom* lady, grifter and actress. She was all big eyes and black hair cut into bangs, a full-bodied bundle of tricks. Lucky had plans for her as well.

But now, with his synapses reconnected, he considered how payback was going to go down.

THE FIRST THING he needed was firepower, and he knew exactly where to go. He purchased two large screwdrivers from Flushing Hardware and called a *see gay*. The driver transported him to Little Italy, the corner of Hester and Mulberry.

The old neighborhood had had its heyday a hundred years back, when it was a haven for new Italian immigrants. Now it was just five blocks of mobbed-up restaurants, cafés, and gift shops, supported by the few thousand Italian old-timers who hadn't long ago escaped to Brooklyn, Staten Island, and Long Island. Now, surrounded on all sides by Chinese *chink* businesses, it was just a barnacle on the hull of the big ship Chinatown.

But for Lucky, it was still where Tony Biondo and what remained of the Campisi crew operated. Tony bought all the Chinese *baak fun* heroin he could get his hands on, and never hesitated to barter weapons for drugs.

At 10 A.M. the Chinese businesses had already begun to bustle with local traffic, while the Italian shops waited impatiently for the tourists. The buildings along Hester Street were quiet, and Lucky knew them well. They were old buildings with a flat stretch of rooftops breaking the skyline. Due to the blind alleyways, the hidden courtyards, the narrow gaps between buildings, and the fire escapes, one could enter a building on Hester and exit from another building on Mulberry, Mott, or Grand Street. The scheme had worked well for generations of mafiosi, but the buildings were now teeming with Chinamen who never fixed the broken door locks at street level.

He entered 98 Hester, made his way up the five flights of tenement stairs. The building was quiet—anyone working had already joined the rat race, and students were long out to school.

The rooftops brought back memories, brought a smirk to his face. Looking down to one of the hidden courtyards, he remembered when there'd been a little tomato patch tended to by an old mafioso. The neighborhood toughs had tormented the Chinese kids then, so Lucky and his friends would urinate off the roof into the capo's garden, laughing at how he was going to make his piss-tomatoes into *gravy, salsa di pomodoro*. "Cheese-eatin' fuckers," he said to himself.

But *this* morning he had a different mission. He crossed the Mulberry rooftops, deserted as usual, toward Grand. Number 300 Mulberry, once a *salumeria* on the street, had had several reincarnations as Chinese restaurants but was now a Chinese supermarket. The metal kitchen exhaust ducts that ran outside up to the roof had long since been abandoned.

He readied the big screwdrivers for the rusted metal plate that covered a section of exhaust fan. The screws were deadlocked, as he'd suspected, but with the two heavy-duty screwdrivers, he pried the plate off easily.

Looking inside the duct, he saw what he'd left there almost a year earlier. *Being prepared. Sun Tzu, always the Boy Scout.* A rubber duffel bag, one of two he'd purchased from the Army Navy Surplus store on Canal Street. He yanked it out, slung its heavy weight off his shoulders.

He left the screwdrivers and carefully stepped back down to the street.

He caught a cab on Canal. The driver was a Pakistani who knew the way to Flushing and didn't ask any other questions. And that was just the way he liked it.

THE HOOKER HOUSE was empty, like he'd figured. Jojo had driven the ladies out to Main Street and they'd be out for the day.

He popped an ecstasy, opened the heavy duffel on Marisol's bed, and pulled the heaviest piece out first. The shotgun, a sawed-off Mossberg 500 with a pistol grip and a folding stock, was six pounds of pure terror. *Needs oil*, he thought. He racked it, loving the metal *chik-cock* sound. Pulled the trigger for a dry *click. Everyone hits the ground.*

The second piece was sexy, a black Uzi nine-millimeter with two twenty-round clips. Not a drive-by ghetto gat, fixed to go full auto if necessary. *Oil,* he thought again. He took a swig from the bottle of brandy on Bettie Bootwang's night table, savoring it as it rushed toward the ecstasy in his blood.

The last pieces were two nine-millimeter semiautomatics, a fancy Beretta, and a throwaway Taurus. He racked and checked the action on both. Except for a metal lunch box, the bottom of the bag was lined with small packs of nine-millimeter ammunition, two boxes of shotgun shells, and a can of oil, all wrapped in cleaning rags.

Inside the lunch box were two fist-sized eight-ounce tubes. He handled them carefully, knowing the stunning power that the military *flash-bang* grenades could generate. *Blow your mind, motherfuckers, make you temporarily deaf, dumb, and blind.* He'd taken them from 61 Mott gambling basement (61M) after a Filipino Marine MP bartered them against a thousand-dollar run of bad luck. *Go Marines,* he sniggered, *the few, the proud.*

He returned them to the lunch box and placed everything back into the rubber duffel. Took another drink from Bettie's bottle. The ecstasy jitterbugged inside him, and he remembered Cigarette Boy and Spareribs, talking shit over his inert body at the hospital. *Dailos* Loy Sung and Taiwan too.

Really, motherfuckers?

He reached for his new disposable cell phone and knew the calls to make.

Thanks But No Thanks

THE CALL CAME in the early morning, as he considered the new workday.

Of course he'd hoped for it, but the intervening five days had dulled Jack's expectation. He wasn't surprised, though, because that was the way Lucky did things, always trying to keep the other side off balance, off guard. He'd been that way since they were kids.

The number wasn't familiar, that too not a surprise. He saved it on redial anyway.

"Yo!" Lucky barked in his A-Dog voice. "Gonna make this short and sweet."

"Go," Jack countered, putting down the half-eaten *cha siew bao* and pressing the cell tighter to his ear.

"Thanks for helping me outta there. That's *it*. Let's say I owe you one."

"Then let's meet. Up on the high ground. You need to come in."

The *high ground*, the term they used for that level stretch of tenement rooftops on Henry Street, across which, as teenagers, they'd stalked and caroused. The flat run allowed them to move from one end of the block to the other, throwing pebbles at the broken-down ghetto windows, dropping water balloons on the rats and cats in the alleys below. Teenage summers spent guzzling Cokes and slurping Icees under the blazing sun, tanning pale Chinese bodies brown.

Later, the Cokes and Icees became beers and weed, as they watched the world change below. There were three of them then, three Chinatown blood brothers. Until Wing Lee got killed that sixteenth summer of their Chinatown lives. *The rooftops full of secrets.*

"Nah," Lucky snorted. "For *what?*"

"Trying to save your life, boy."

"*Again* with the '*witless* protection'?" Medicated contempt in his voice. "You mean *rat* everyone out and I get to run an egg-roll stand somewhere? Change my name? Paper ID? Ha! *Giving* me what they put our grandfathers in jail for?"

"Whoa, slow down, Mr. Historian."

"I have to kill someone before they wanna protect me? Wanna make me a paper son?"

"You can request a *location*, Tat."

"Sure. Any place that's *nowhere*, right? I'd rather die, bro."

"There's that death wish talking again. Let's roll it back . . ."

"You don't get it, Jacky boy. *Forward's* all I got. I ain't waiting to die somewhere selling takeout."

"Yeah, why waste time, right?"

"Funny. You got jokes."

"Funny like a funeral."

"Ha ha ha."

"Funny like you in a ditch."

"Ha ha."

"In a back alley somewhere."

"Never gonna happen."

"In a box going to a potter's field."

"You watchin' too many Hong Kong movies, boy."

"No one cares. No one visits. In a year, no one even remembers who the fuck you were."

"Like they'll remember you? Yellow-face hero cop? Running-dog chump for the *gwai lo* white boys?"

"You're suicidal. Guess that's why they call you guys Ghosts."

"I just came back from the dead. I got a second chance and you want me to disappear?"

"A second chance for *what*? To get killed for good this time?"

"Be real. Me disappearing's gonna close some of your cases?"

"It's a limited-time offer, Tat."

"Limited time's all I got, bro."

"C'mon, let's meet on the high ground."

"Tell you what—I get the chance, I'll come by your crib. What's the address?"

Jack hesitated, not because he didn't trust Lucky but because it sounded like he was blowing him off. He knew it might be his last shot, so he gave Lucky his Sunset Park address.

"See ya around, kid," Lucky laughed.

"Wait . . ." Jack asked of the dial tone. His connection to Lucky now deader than ever.

2 Lucky

TWO MOTT STREET, a sixteen-story mirrored-glass triangle, was barely twenty years old, a *modern* Chinatown building. It sat on the corner of Mott and Chatham Square, along the north-south thoroughfare that led down into the Seaport and the Financial District.

It was a professional building anchored by the busiest branch of Citibank in Chinatown. On the upper levels were doctors' offices, dentists, accountants, immigration lawyers, and travel agencies.

Wedged into the corner of the shiny stone and tile lobby was a small counter where Ah Fai, the janitor who doubled as part-time security, stood observing the people as they came and went on the elevators. He was there only a couple of hours a day during the rush, a make-work *ceremonial* post. Getting unfamiliar clients, patients, and contractors to sign the counter log was a hit-or-miss proposition, especially when groups of people entered the building, invariably bound for the travel agencies and immigration lawyers. Building management considered the building safe, and they weren't willing to pay for full-time legitimate security.

Everything was recorded on a closed-circuit surveillance system anyway.

Ah Fai checked his watch and waited for noon to end the shift.

THE LOTUS PEARL café was crowded with locals enjoying their *cheung fun* and *baos*, reading Chinese newspapers and freebie magazines. No one paid much attention to the two workmen in blue coveralls and hard hats, sipping their cardboard cups of *nai cha*, heads down at the end of the narrow counter along the window wall. Between them was a canvas tool bag and a coil of white cable wire.

A woman in a black bubble coat sat on a stool at the other end, nursing a cup of *ning mung cha*. She wore black Wayfarers that shielded her eyes, which were looking toward the building across the way. *2 Mott Street*.

The workmen noticed a *van jai* pulling up at the corner curb and discharging a group of travelers with rolling luggage. *Yau haak* tourists.

The woman in the black coat exited the Lotus Pearl as the tour group headed toward the mirrored building.

Leaving their teas on the counter, the two hard hats also left the café.

It was almost noon.

AH FAI WATCHED them enter the lobby, young people jabbering in Mandarin. *Obnoxious*, he thought with Cantonese prejudice. *Probably heading for Taiwan Tours on the sixth floor*. They barely paid him any mind as they passed.

Behind them a few steps, a woman wearing black

sunglasses was unzipping her black coat. *Ming sing like a movie star.* He was admiring the little black dress she wore underneath as she slowly headed his way.

He was preparing to be helpful when her high heels wobbled and slid, causing her to lurch forward, spilling contents from her handbag onto the floor in front of him.

"Oh my god!" she cried. "*Sooo* embarrassing!" He saw a makeup kit, lipsticks, nail polish, a tampon, and a gold foil sheet of condoms. When she bent and kneeled to retrieve the scattered items, the minidress rode up her thighs and her breasts threatened to overflow the top.

Ah Fai was mesmerized, kneeling to help her as she scooped up lipsticks and nail polish.

"You were going to *which* office?" he asked, smiling his best smile, tucking the condoms back into her handbag. He barely noticed the two men wearing blue hard hats, waving a clipboard at him as they passed. *Contractors, going to the manager's office*, he thought as his eyes went back to her breasts.

"You know, I actually think I'm in the wrong building," she said, straightening up. "Let me make sure. But thanks so much anyway." His heart sank as he watched her exit the building, looking briefly back at the facade before stepping out of sight.

He took a breath, his attention divided between the tour group *probably on six* and hoping the sexy lady in black would come back.

The two blue hard hats who'd gone upstairs couldn't have been further from his mind.

* * *

THE SMALLEST ROOM on the eighth floor was a money drop disguised as a sales office. There was a chair-and-desk setup with a phone and a computer monitor. A wall shelf of catalogs featuring products from mainland China. The products *actually* involved were untaxed cigarettes, contraband counterfeits, and stolen alcohol, collateral proceeds from the gambling dens on Mott Street.

Charley Joe sat at the desk, calming his craving for Hop Lee's Cantonese crab and lobster, which he planned to order for lunch.

Dup Choy sat on the only other piece of furniture, a knockoff designer couch. He considered lighting a bootleg Cohiba and pissing off the entire eighth floor again.

The knock at the door caught their attention. *The cartons of untaxed Marlboros promised by Cigarette Boy,* thought Charley, rising from behind the desk. He patted his pockets for his lighter as Choy opened the door.

They were surprised to see the two workmen wearing blue hard hats. *Both Chinese,* observed Choy as he pocketed the Cohiba. The men drew guns from their coveralls and shoved their way inside.

Before Choy could form the words *Lucky* and *Jojo,* a gun barrel slammed him across the side of his head. He was reeling, seeing reds and blacks even as the second blow broke his nose. A hoof kick to his balls took the wind out of him and dropped him onto the couch. He couldn't see through the pain that Jojo had a gun pressed to the back of Charley's comb-over.

"Open the safe!" Lucky barked as he pistol-whipped Dup Choy again, sending bits of gum and teeth across the floor. Choy, the On Yee enforcer, reduced to a bloody whimpering mess.

Charley Joe fell to his knees in terror, shaky fingers on the safe's dial. Jojo, with a grin on his face, tossed Lucky a pair of swinging handcuffs. *A pimp product from the bondage trunk of tricks*. He had a second pair for Charley.

Lucky pressed a knee into the back of Choy's head and cuffed him, hands behind, through the armrest of the couch.

"You'll never get away with this," Charley said, trembling as he swung the safe door open. Jojo cuffed him to the desk as Lucky scooped the safe's contents into the tool bag. They left Dup Choy bleeding on the couch and headed for the stairwell.

It took them only a moment to get down to the street.

AT THE EDGE of the Seventh Precinct on the Lower East Side, Jack was at the end of an assisted case, translating and explaining to the uniforms on scene how the Fujianese grandmother they'd responded to had just gotten scammed out of her life savings. A Chinese man-and-woman con team was working the area.

The emergency call had been patched through the Fifth Precinct—*2 Mott Street Room 808. Possible assault.* He was within a five-minute straight shot down the

Bowery to Chinatown, but the patrol car he'd badged, flashing lights and whooping sirens, got him there even faster.

There was nobody in the lobby of 2 Mott as he took an elevator to the eighth floor. Room 808, according to the floor plan on the elevator wall, was at the end of the L-shaped corridor. A stairway in between.

Down the corridor, what sounded like a commotion made him pause, brush back his hand against the Colt on his hip, before turning that corner. He heard, "It was Lucky. That motherfucker!" in angry Toishanese. "Put *yit mon* ten thousand on his head!"

"Shut the fuck up!" a second voice yelled. Something overturned and a crash thumped. He thought he'd heard those voices before. *At the hospital.*

"And that faggot Jojo too! *Yit mon* each!"

"*Dew nei louh mouh* motherfucker, where's that idiot from downstairs?"

Before Jack could move, a handyman rushed past him carrying a big bolt cutter. Jack turned the corner behind him and watched him go into No. 808.

Charley Joe was barking "*Lun yeung* idiot! Who asked you to call 911?"

"*Duey m'jee!*" Ah Fai kowtowed. "Sorry, but I saw all the blood, and *he* was moaning."

"Cut the cuffs off! Hurry!"

Jack stepped into the doorway, saw Dup Choy on the couch, just a beaten bloody face. To his right, the handyman chopping off the handcuffs chaining

Charley Joe to the overturned table. There was a safe that was partly open.

He pushed aside the man and used his own handcuff key to free Dup Choy, who fell silent.

"You were saying?" Jack smiled.

"Fuck you," Charley Joe said, cuing Dup Choy. "We got nothing to say. He slipped and fell." Choy angrily spat out a bloody clot.

"Lucky and Jojo?" Jack pressed.

"Shut the fuck up," Charley warned Dup Choy as he slammed his chopped handcuffs to the floor. "And *you* get the fuck out of my office before I call the *real* cops."

EMS techs appeared in the doorway, saw bloody Choy.

"He had an accident," Charley Joe said in his good Chinatown English. "Could use some cleaning up."

The emergency techs prepped some first aid and the handyman gladly left the office. Jack thought about sur-veillance tapes and eye-fucked Charley on the way out.

"*Ha chi la,*" warned Jack. "Next time."

"I'll be waiting, *lun yeung,*" Charley spat, "cop prick."

THE CLOSED-CIRCUIT SYSTEM ended in the man-agement office, where they reused and reloaded the videotapes.

The building manager's office was on the seventeenth floor, which was really the sixteenth floor, Jack knew, because Chinese high-rises didn't designate the four-teenth floors. The Chinese numbers for 14, *yat say*, were synonymous with *certain death,* so no Chinese would ever lease on that floor.

Just below the roof, the manager's corner office had floor-to-ceiling windows, a great view of lower Manhattan spreading out from Chatham Square and the Chinatown rooftops below. For a moment, Jack imagined neighborhood teenagers running across those rooftops.

The building manager was absent, but his assistant seemed concerned at the sight of Jack's badge and was happy to cooperate. He rewound all the tapes back a half hour as Jack instructed. The incident was *fresh* and Jack wanted to see how two assailants had gotten access to Charley Joe's office.

The assistant left him at the TV monitors and Jack reviewed the grainy black-and-white videotape. From the lobby view he saw how lax security was, people coming and going without any restriction. Typical for commercial buildings in Chinatown.

He saw the handyman who'd rushed to the office. *Ah Fai,* they'd called him. There was a group going by, mostly women, pausing for the elevators.

He was looking for two men, Lucky and another man named Jojo. A woman entered, stumbled, and spilled her handbag. She stooped to the floor, and Ah Fai assists her as two workmen pass them by.

He rewound the lobby view, watched it again.

The group goes by, followed by a lone woman.

The woman stumbles.

Ah Fai helps her pick up items from the floor.

Two workmen in hard hats pass by, heading for the elevators. The lone woman scoops up her belongings and leaves the building. She exits to the left, toward Chatham Square. Ah Fai is alone in the lobby.

He cued the elevator tapes for the time stamp. There were three elevators, designated by numbers 1, 2, 3. The group of travelers entered No. 1. Door closes, and floor indicator shows sixth-floor destination.

Several office workers ride down No. 2 and exit to the street-level lobby.

The two workmen take No. 3, exit onto the eighth floor.

He rewound the tapes and refocused. *The group of ladies exits onto the sixth floor. Elevator No. 2 sits empty in the lobby on call.* The two hard hats in No. 3, keeping their heads low, huddle over a tool bag. Their bodies block the view as they transfer something into their coveralls. They exit on eight, going left in the direction of Room 808.

The elevator views showed nothing unusual for the next ten minutes. Office workers heading down to lunch, slowing the elevators as they stopped on almost every floor. The two workmen never reappeared on any of the elevators.

He realized it clearly then. *If they were fleeing a crime scene, would they wait for an elevator during the lunch-hour rush?* There were no cameras in the stairway, just the one view on the roof door and another where the stairs exited out to the lobby.

No one exited to the roof. On the second tape he saw

people, mostly impatient workers from the lower floors, exiting into the lobby. Several minutes into the tape, he saw them, *the two hard hats going through the stairwell door into the lobby*. He checked the time stamp and synced the lobby tape to it. The view showed the two men exiting the building, turning left toward Chatham Square. *12:03* P.M. He never got a good look at their faces, just the tops of their hard hats.

He narrowed his eyes and focused on the time line.

At 11:46 A.M. a group of travelers enters the lobby. Followed by a lone woman a few steps behind. At 11:49 two workmen enter the lobby, take elevator No. 3 to the eighth floor. At 12:02 P.M. the call comes in to 911—a woman from one of the eighth-floor offices. Reported that she heard *yelling*. At 12:03 a call from the mainte-nance-room extension. A garbled report in broken English, presumably Ah Fai. At 12:03 the two hard hats exit from the stairwell through the lobby.

At 12:05 he'd gotten the patch-through message from the Fifth Precinct to respond to 2 Mott. He saw himself enter the lobby at 12:07, take Elevator No. 1 to the eighth floor.

Figuring for the time line and reviewing the tapes, they'd already had a half-hour head start on him.

Looking out the tall windows, he appreciated this piece of lower Manhattan. Two streets to the right of Chatham Square sat the hulking block of police head-quarters, One Police Plaza. *Not the direction in which two guys who'd just committed a crime would go*. He began to see

Lucky's scheme more clearly than any videotape could show.

Two blocks to the north, the Manhattan Bridge led the way to Brooklyn or Queens. *Park a car outside Confucius Towers. Or take one of the see gays who hang out near there.* Or even a minivan *sai ba* to Flushing.

No videotape was going to show them dropping their hard hats into the corner garbage at Catherine Street, or chucking the clipboard and the coil of cable on the other side of Division. But he saw it all with a wicked clarity, knowing Lucky as he did.

He also wondered how the call had come his way.

If Captain Marino wanted a report, he wasn't going to like the one he was going to get. *Officially,* he'd responded to the 2 Mott location to find one injured man bleeding about the head and face and another man apparently unhurt. *They* declined help from NYPD, stating that the injured party had fallen and would be treated by local doctor(s). *They* declined EMS aid beyond First Aid, and claimed that the 911 Emergency calls were *inadvertent* and incorrect.

The woman in the adjacent office who called 911 stated that she heard angry yelling but couldn't make out the context because of the different dialects. She had feared a fight was occurring.

The janitor offered conflicting statements and then refused to comment further.

The EMS report would indicate *lacerations to the head, a broken nose, and broken teeth.* All of which could have occurred as a result of a fall. *Patient aided and EMS departed as TPO.*

He didn't have any proof that an assault occurred and only knew of Lucky's involvement through what he overheard in the corridor outside the office. If Charley Joe and Dup Choy weren't going to press charges, intending to take matters into their own hands, then there was no crime to report. Just another Chinatown dodge.

The answers to the questions he had for Lucky weren't in Manhattan, he knew. He left 2 Mott for Confucius Towers Parking. With the Mustang gunning through Queens, he'd arrive in Flushing Chinatown in twenty minutes.

The One-O-Nine

THOUSANDS OF CHINESE, Koreans, Indians and Pakistanis passing by as he parked the Mustang. Main Street looking like a foreign port.

The 109th Precinct covered all of Flushing China-town, including Main Street, Lucky's last known destination. He was also looking for an accomplice named Jojo.

When he punched up the precinct's CompStat reports the number of incidents followed the categories of homicide, assaults, robbery, vice, gang-related and other bullets. When he narrowed it to Asian businesses and organizations the numbers shrank. No killings recently but robbery and assaults rising, probably aided by a gang-related upsurge. He didn't see anything with Lucky's footprints.

He ran the aka for "Jojo" and found none.

The Organized Crime Control Bureau, OCCB, listed some familiar names under Asian organized crime groups: Hip Ching Benevolent Association, On Yee Merchants Association, Fook Hing Benevolent Society, Taiwanese Big Bamboo, even the Mumbai Mafia. Their street soldiers wearing the tags of the Black Dragons, Ghost

Legion, Fuk Ching Boys, Seoul Power, Mumbai Mob, and Bamboo Circle.

He knew Lucky was in a hotbed, but when he ran Jojo's tag he again came up empty.

Plenty of yellow crime, though.

There were a lot of Chinese nearby in Jackson Heights and Elmhurst, mostly those Chinatown families who could afford to or had saved enough money, following the subway lines out to Queens in the exodus that began in the 1970s. The formerly white communities welcomed, absorbed them. *Out of the Chinatown tenements at last, and only a dozen stops, a half hour on the subway back for bok choy, fresh fish, and flank steak.*

Nowadays Chinese supermarkets and shopping malls had made everything available in those communities. The only reason to take the subway back was to visit those they'd left behind, and for the crowds on Chinese New Year's Day.

He ran CompStat for the Heights and Elmhurst, the 110th Precinct, as well.

Familiar names again, the Hip Ching and the On Yee Associations, both old-school and old-line Chinatown organized crime following the expansion of their turf into Queens. *Any of Lucky's connections could help him here also.* Mostly incidences of illegal mah-jongg parlors and high-stakes poker games, casino nights at karaoke clubs. ATF violations for untaxed cigarettes and alcohol. *Interesting crimes but no Jojo.*

When he stroked the OCCB database for JOJO, he hit

a trifecta; there were *three* aka JoJos. One African-American, *Joe "JoJo" Johnson*; one Hispanic, *Johnny "Jojo" Cespedes*; and one Chinese, *Man Tit Yang* aka "JoJo" or "Jojo Yang."

Two years earlier, the OCCB raided an On Yee massage parlor in Elmhurst, in the course of which they arrested one Man Tit Yang aka Jojo, for pandering, possession of forged instruments (credit cards), and resisting arrest.

From his NYS driver's license, a picture of him emerged. A handsome guy with an edgy face, he was thirty-six years old. *A low-level playa, a wannabe mack.* From the name, Jack knew he was Chiu Chao, probably a member of the Fook Hing, a smaller subset of the On Yee tong.

According to the listings in the Chinese Chamber of Commerce there were twelve massage parlors within the confines of the 109th Precinct and another twelve in the adjacent 110th. Many of them were listed as spas. He knew he wouldn't have the time to check them all out. He could catch a call from Manhattan South and didn't want to get caught out too long on a no-case. But at least he had a picture now.

Jojo had pleaded out to the pandering, paid a fine. The bogus credit cards were tossed because a judge saw *illegal search and seizure*. The charge of resisting arrest was dropped.

Arrested along with him was one Jadine Jung, a Canadian Chinese former runaway from Vancouver. She was twenty-six years old, her mug shot, otherwise a naturally pretty face, almost a scowl.

The driver's license had an Elmhurst address for Jojo, ten minutes back down the highway toward Manhattan.

If he could find Jojo, he'd find Lucky.

When he got back to the car his cell phone vibrated in his pocket. The number looked vaguely familiar but he let it go to message. *Schedule an appointment?* It was May McCann.

Oh, hell no, he was thinking, as he fired up the Mustang.

Crib

THE STUDIO WAS a far cry from the hooker hostel in New Hyde Park. A mini loft with wood floors, a stainless steel kitchen wall, a bathroom with stone vanity and tub. He sat on a luxe armchair in the middle of the big room, opposite a media wall of flat-screen TV and CD stereo.

Images danced across the muted TV screen. He had a CD playing low key, a sax medley.

He finished the little pipe bowl of sinsemilla and let it play out to ashes. The potent weed calmed him, brought his thoughts around to Sun Tzu's greatest hits. *All warfare is deception.* He knew to plan ahead. *Stay on the move. A small force can defeat a large force.* Taking another swallow from the tumbler of XO, he scanned the room.

At the far end was a sleeping area, a full futon mattress screened off behind black wood Chinese panels. There was a picture window there, overlooking the low-rise rooftops of Main Street across the expressway.

He kept the rubber duffel of weapons there.

The model studio apartment at Asia Manor was the perfect hideaway for him, tucked away at the edge of Flushing but close enough to strike anywhere in the city. He'd dropped five thousand cash on the sales manager's desk for a one-month lease. *He didn't think he'd need it longer than that.*

Asia Manor, a twenty-one-story condominium development, was funded by investment from China and South Asia. It had recently opened with only a third of the condos sold, mostly on the upper levels. *In a partially occupied building, there'd be less chance of anyone recognizing him.*

He avoided the eighth floor, which he knew would be full of nosy Chinese. *The less anyone saw of his comings and goings the better.*

There was a parking area behind the building, where he kept the '88 Buick Regal that he bought off a used lot on the island. Cash. Hit da road, no questions asked. *Put ya money on the table an' drive it off the lot.* The salesman was happy to get rid of the gas guzzler, but Lucky knew the car had power to spare, and he wasn't concerned about the cost of gas. Cruising was like sitting in a lounge chair driving a battering ram. Better than any lightweight speedster. It reminded him of the black Sabre and how Lefty—he still couldn't believe that Lefty was dead, gone, not remembering any of it—how he used to muscle that car through Chinatown, scattering the tourists who clogged the streets. Or when they had to shoot drive-bys against the Fukienese, with Kongo, the big Malay, riding shotgun. *Also dead.*

He had a war wagon now, just in need of another driver, another shooter in the scattergun seat. *He'd find them soon enough.*

He swallowed a tab of ecstasy and washed it down with a gulp of XO. The speed helped him refocus, brought a dark energy back into his blood. He killed the TV and opened the tool bag they'd used for the 2 Mott job. Inside was what was left of the thirty-two thousand he took from Charley Joe's safe. Counting the leftovers, he felt like calling Charley to let him know he was short twenty thousand, and there'd be no *fuhgeddaboudit. Come back and bust your head open like I did Dup Choy.*

Out of the dirty cash, he'd given five thousand to Jojo, *not bad for twenty minutes' sidekick work,* and two thousand to Jadine, *easy pay for two minutes of stumbling and flashing her tits.* Better than sucking and fucking four *fat hom sup los* at five hundred a pop.

He gave five hundred each to Bettie, Marisol, and Ah Won jeer, the hos in the hostel, for bringing him back to life. They were sad to see him go.

Where you gonna go, honey?

Don't worry about it. I'll be in touch.

Promise, baby?

Bet on it.

He didn't go far, just to the edge of Flushing. And the eighteen thousand he had left was enough for the roundup posse he had in mind. He closed the tool bag and stashed it under the futon mattress. From the window he could see the lights in the distance, coming alive in the sunset.

He finished the last of the XO and chambered a round in the Beretta. Accustomed to rolling half-cocked, he headed for the Regal, and the night lights calling.

The meet with Loo Ga, first up, took him south. On the side streets of Rego Park, he passed a Hasidic seminary, some Hasids on civilian patrol, and came to the avenue. Parking across from the Canton Gourmet, he was twenty minutes early.

The Canton Gourmet had a long red wall that reflected off the mirrored wall opposite. A giant lacquered Chinese fan adorned the wall, and a row of blacktop tables led to the spot he chose in the back, where he could watch the door.

During the dead hours before the dinner rush, the place was empty.

"*Dung yun*," he advised. "I'm waiting for someone."

The waiter brought a cup of tea and a menu and left him alone. He observed how the restaurant operated. The Canton Gourmet was one of eight Chinese restaurants run citywide by the "Canton Group" of the On Yee Merchants Association. The Group was protected by the Ghost Legion in this part of Queens, under a lesser *dailo*, probably Kid Taiwan, or Spanish Loy Sung.

While Lucky bossed over the lucrative gambling basements on Mott Street and money schemes throughout Chinatown, *dailos* in Queens grabbed whatever they could get. Extorting Chinese restaurants, massage parlors, and karaoke bars was a good racket, until the *protection* was actually needed.

He was sure nobody here would know, or recognize, them.

Over the steamy tea, he remembered.

* * *

LOO GA WAS ex-Ghost, once a rising star then drummed out when things started going bad on his watch. Contraband missing. Deals gone bad. Some suspected sabotage from within his own crew.

When a truckload of cigarettes got hijacked, he got blamed for it. When Loy Sung pitched a bitch he took the brunt. But before all that, he'd mentored Lucky after Wing Lee's killing, before Lucky's own meteoric rise in the Ghost Legion.

Now all he had was Chinese numbers from Long Island City, and a high-stakes Chinese poker game in Sunset Park. Pocket money that kept the pokers warm.

He was *Loo* Hakka Chinese, but they called him Luga, because he carried a Luger, a nine-millimeter parabellum German Luger, and was a big fan of the Nazis. He didn't know from the politics, just white people hating and killing other white people. He wasn't wearing an armband but did carry a gunmetal Zippo lighter with a swastika on one side and a war eagle on the other.

The Luger was a vintage midnight blue Walther P-38 Auto Pistol imported from Germany. It was a five-inch piece that could spit out eight shots of nine-millimeter deadheads. An ounce of quick death.

Loo Ga liked to show it off, especially around the ladies. Except there were no ladies now, none in exile.

He'd be interested in what *dailo* Lucky would suggest— a quick hit, a big share. And more important, revenge against *dailos* Loy Sung and Kid Taiwan, who'd thrown him under the bus.

Loo Ga arrived not a minute late, looking thicker than Lucky remembered but still an imposing figure. He stepped directly to the table and sat down without a word. The waiter followed with a cup of tea and Lucky ordered chicken wings and spareribs just to have some finger food on the table.

Loo Ga didn't speak until the waiter left them.

"Been a while, kid."

"Yeah, how's tricks?"

"I'm getting by. You?"

"I'm putting together a crew."

"Yeah?"

"Gonna bust a few moves. Bust some heads, too."

"Yeah."

"Still got that Luger?"

"Sure." He patted his hip.

"So you wanna ride shotgun?"

"Maybe."

"All I hear is *yeah* and *maybe*. Maybe like *what?*"

"Maybe like who else you got in the posse?"

"Maybe that ain't none of your business yet?"

"Fair enough."

"But no worries. No *scumbags* in this crew." Loo Ga knew who Lucky was referring to.

"Gonna take back Chinatown?" he smirked.

"You don't think so?"

"I heard you were dead."

"I look dead to you?" After a moment, a felonius smile came across Loo Ga's face.

"I'm *in*. Just no jerkoffs, okay?"

"No jerkoffs," as the waiter returned with the finger food.

He was already thinking of the next meet.

HE DROVE THROUGH Woodside, once Irish Catholic, now mostly Dominican and Central American. He cruised the Regal down Northern Boulevard and found a spot two blocks from the Golden Village.

The Golden Village had a softer look than the Canton Gourmet, simple wood tones and beige walls. A big black-and-white photo-blowup of a Chinese village filled one wall. A lone customer, who looked like a student, sat at a front table slurping wonton noodles while doing homework.

One lady cashier, one middle-aged waiter. Not much clamor from the kitchen in the back.

He took a small table near the kitchen where he could see the front door. The waiter brought a menu, left him to peruse it. He ignored it and thought about Say Low. A momentary sense of sadness swept through him but he couldn't remember the shootout everyone says happened.

Say Low, *little brother*, was deceased Lefty's kid brother. Now in his twenties, he was a kid no more. Even back then, he'd been a better driver than Lefty, but big brother caved to the pleas of their mother and kept Say Low out of the Ghost Legion, out of Chinatown gang life.

But Lefty was gone now, and soon, mom would be crying about losing another son to the life.

Say Low had hung out with other street racers on Cross Bay Boulevard, with the Drag Boyz through Howard Beach mobbed Queens. Dangerous races along the Long Island border. He drove souped-up cars and picked up pretty women. But *life in the fast lane* was a costly style he hadn't had the cash to carry off as a part-time limo driver.

He'd been a Ghost wannabe for a long time.

Tonight, Lucky thought, *he was going to get his chance to jump in.*

Say Low stepped toward the table, a wiry-looking young man wearing racing leather and a fingerless glove on one hand. Hair cut sharp like he was a living anime or K-pop character. He quietly sat, staring at Lucky like he was the resurrection and new life.

"My brother was like you," he smiled, "a legend." Lucky nodded his agreement, letting him continue.

"And a great driver. And that's what I want to do. You said I would only *drive.* Because I don't want to carry. Promised mom I wouldn't do that."

Lucky quickly dispatched the waiter with an order of dumplings and scallion pancakes for the table.

"No guns, no drugs, no mule. Just *drive,* that's all I want to do."

Spoken like a prima donna, thought Lucky, if he didn't know better, that the Ghosts had already cost one brother, broken a family. *Sure, he'd be cleaner than no prints.* But the car was going to carry *any fuckin' thing* Lucky needed.

The waiter returned with the hot plates.

"Enjoy the dumplings, kid," Lucky grinned. "And welcome aboard."

THE CANTON PALACE brought him to Jackson Heights, *Little India*. He parked down the block from the Sari Shop, away from the Lakshmi Temple.

Again, the red wall, the big glossy Chinese fan. *A franchise logo*, he mused, again taking a table near the kitchen. Except for a couple waiting for takeout, the place was empty. He observed one cashier, one manager, one waiter. Only the helper *da jop* working in the kitchen.

The lone waiter brought him tea and a menu, then left him.

He watched the door and waited for Cowboy.

Cowboy, *ah Ngow*, had once bossed a top crew of Chinese laborers who renovated older buildings all over Chinatown. He knew the ins and outs of the labyrinths of the neighborhoods' hidden buildings, and was suspected of having master keys to every building on Mott Street and most of Bayard.

His two big sins were gambling and young girls. Risking thousands on the flip of a card, on the rattle of fan-tan buttons. Risking perversion with girls barely seventeen, trafficked trix.

He'd lost his car, a Land Rover, in a rigged game of

Chinese thirteen-card poker. The Chinese House had provided bottomless alcohol, and diversions like young-looking girls serving the Johnny Walker. The high-stakes hustle was a Ghost card game in Elmhurst, with Queens *dailo* Hammer using a bottom dealer in a fixed game.

In the ensuing alcoholic haze, Cowboy couldn't prove anything and bitterly swallowed the loss of his car. He would harbor bad feelings against the Queens Ghosts, Lucky knew.

His other sin was the *desire* he'd brought back from a sex junket to Bangkok, *a lust for young girls*. In Chinatown his reputation preceded him, his preferences well known. Fat Lily's had her youngest ones, still in their twenties, dress up like schoolgirls. Angelina Chao was known to fly in an over-seventeen *kit leui* kitten just for *that* crowd. But even the hard-core pussy chasers shunned him, a *pervert* in their noble womanizing midst.

Cowboy was also known as a good Hung-style fighter, but in the age of the gun, *what good was kung fu fighting?* Still, having skills was better than gangsters with no training.

The man had issues, Lucky knew, but he also had the right motivation and could be key to the comeback. Besides, a big payday and a bonus of a round trip back to Bangkok would no doubt interest him.

A thickset Toishanese man filled the doorway of the Canton Palace. He glanced at the waiter and nodded in Lucky's direction. The waiter quickly jotted down Lucky's order of a plate of *see jup* chicken and noodles, and steak *kow*, as the big man settled his bulk at the table.

Nothing like a good meal to whet ah Ngow's appetite for bigger adventures.

Cowboy didn't have the gift of gab and seemed to know he was there to listen. In the time it took for the food to arrive at the table, Lucky had reviewed the setup they'd discussed. He watched as the big man lit into the plates of steak and chicken, remembering that he didn't need Cowboy just for his muscle and motivation.

Cowboy liked the images of fresh money and young pussy.

As the food disappeared, Lucky wasn't surprised at Cowboy's answer.

"When do we start?" he said, grinning. "I'm in it to win it."

THE LAST MEET turned him back toward Shea Stadium, to a beer-and-burger joint named Tommy's Place Pub.

He parked under the elevated tracks.

Tommy's Place was a sports bar, catering to the fans after ballgames at Shea. The big room was all deep blues and dark woods, booths and tables surrounding an oval bar in the middle.

Mets team posters and orange banners covered the walls. A blowup of Tom Seaver in that golden year.

At 9 P.M. on a Tuesday night, the place was almost empty. He chose a big table near the back of the house where he could see everything and where three men could spread out comfortably. *Nothing unusual, just three Chinamen having beers on a dead night with no ballgame.*

Waited.

He'd once supplied the ecstasy and weed, the eight balls that the Lam brothers sold out of the bars and karaoke clubs in College Point. Until *dailo* Loy Sung got wind of it and his crew of Elmhurst Ghosts took over the action, freezing them out.

They'd been muscled out to just two bottle clubs near Bayside, dealing quarters of weed and oxy tabs to the club kids.

Lucky figured them to be interested. It wasn't like their criminal careers had taken off.

Whoa, dailo wants us in? they'd repeated to themselves. *No fuckin' kiddin'?*

They both had U.S. Army experience, tall Lam serving in Germany, the other in Korea. *Weapons and training.* What they also brought back stateside, however, was knowing how bar clubs operated, and how to deal the party drugs that Lucky's crew had fronted.

They came in separately, the shorter one first. Looked around, spotted Lucky and came his way.

The taller Lam stepped in and scanned the lightly attended bar scene. He followed a few steps back, to Lucky's table. The tall brother, the silent one.

The shorter brother, enthusiastic and excitable, spoke for the two of them.

"If we can get back in the action," he said too eagerly, "then we're in." Tall Lam nodded, cracking a smile that was more like a grimace.

"Deal," Lucky replied, signaling the waitress for a round of beers. He handed his phone to Short Lam.

"Get in my cell," he commanded quietly.

As Short Lam punched in their telephone numbers, Tall Lam finally spoke, his words tinged with awe.

"They said you were *dead* . . ."

Lucky just smiled and nodded. *Blind faith*, he reflected, had to count for something.

BACK AT ASIA Manor, he unstrapped the Beretta, took a gulp of XO, and collected his thoughts. He'd recruited some hard-core players, *untested*, he knew, but they'd be tested soon enough. *He, who'd once bossed a crew of twenty-four full-blooded Ghosts and another fifty Hong Kong crazies on the streets. He, who'd ruled the ten-block square from Mulberry to Chrystie, Bayard to Delancey. A quarter-million cash a month in gambling and drugs alone. Just a small piece of the big Chinatown pie. He, now putting together a crazy crew of eight—Lucky's Eight—he was beginning to like the sound of it.*

Besides, it wasn't like he could just form an ace crew right away and resume his status as *dailo*. But now the best he could muster was a pimp and a prostitute, a pervert, a prima donna, a bitter ex-Ghost, and a pair of military drug-dealing brothers. Worse than a motley crew, this rogue collection. *They weren't outcasts for nothing.*

But they all fit in Lucky's scheme, to posse up a new crew of crazies, misfits, and desperadoes with old beefs against the On Yee and the Ghost Legion, all motivated righteously by revenge and profit. *Like a hijack-and-rip-off swat team.*

He popped the clip out of the Beretta, fired up some sinsemilla. He unloaded and rearranged the bullets in the clip. A couple of tokes was all he needed and he closed his eyes.

Attack when they don't expect you.

A dogfight came to mind, *bloody bulls in a big pit, tearing each other to bits. The On Yee, and the triads, betting on the outcome. Alpha dogs alla dem.*

He slipped the clip back in and racked a round. Thumbed the safety on.

Know how to use a small force.

He leaned back in the luxe chair and imagined the Lucky Eight, banging their way back into the big game . . .

Spa

THE ELMHURST CHINESE link led to a two-family house in a row of low-rises on a suburban bedroom street. Aromatics of Chinese cooking wafting from the houses. Jack tried to imagine Jojo living in this *eyeball* community; *everyone sees what everyone else is up to.*

"*Fei jor la!*" the Chinese landlady exclaimed. "He skipped out six months ago, the *say yun tau*. Still owes me two months' rent!"

"I need to see his room."

"It's cleaned out. He left a TV and a piece of luggage."

"You have them?"

"In the garage. It's empty."

When he checked the luggage he discovered a Chinese magazine in the side panel of the rollaway. The bulk-mail label bore a massage-parlor address for the Temple Garden Spa, Elmhurst.

Another Chinese rub joint, Jack knew, trying to figure the connection when his phone jangled. A Chinatown number, *the Fifth Precinct dispatch?*

"Detective Yu?" a female voice.

"Yes."

"Respond to One-Seven-Five Hester Street."

"Copy. What's there?"

"M1A. Missing Person, need language assist. Apartment Four D."

"Copy that," he said into dial tone, imagining the bridge and the cruise back into Chinatown.

Forget Me Not

ONE SEVENTY-FIVE HESTER was a squat four-story tenement near the end of the block. He parked the Mustang out front and climbed the metal stairs that ran between a florist's shop and a mini pharmacy.

He caught his breath when he got to the fourth floor, scanning for 4D, one of the four apartments on each floor. In the dim light of the bare bulb in the hallway, he could see 4C written in marker on one door. The other door bore no markings. He knocked on it.

The old Chinese lady had to be seventy years old. She was guilt-ridden and racked with worry.

"*Lo gung yew chi gnoy beng,*" she said in her guttural Toishanese. *Husband has Alzheimer's.*

"It's all my fault," she said despairingly. She clenched and unclenched her fists as he made a few mental notes. *A rundown one-bedroom apartment, typical of Chinatown's old housing stock.* But *clean,* the way old folks are neat and keep everything in place.

"He was watching *En see,* TV, as usual, so I went to prepare dinner."

"He just left?"

"When I came out of the kitchen—it was only ten

minutes—he was gone. The TV was playing but he was gone." He took a long *shaolin* breath, noticed the moldy muskiness of the room, and let her continue.

"I panicked. I went straight up to the roof but he wasn't there. I looked down to make sure he hadn't fallen." *Or jumped,* thought Jack.

"I ran downstairs. Looked up and down *Hee-see Da gaai.* But didn't see him. I checked around the building area." She started to tremble. "He's nowhere to be found!"

"Calm down," Jack said. "Has he done this before?"

"Only once but that was out on the street. We were shopping for *gwa choy* vegetables when he wandered off."

"You called 911?"

"When?"

"Now."

"Yes. They found someone who speaks some Toisha-nese." He wasn't surprised how the assist call came his way.

"It's all my fault," she repeated.

"You may want to post some fliers," he suggested. "Pictures."

"Pictures?" She frowned. "I don't have a camera." He could tell she was confused.

"You can post pictures around Chinatown. With a telephone number so people can call you."

"*En wah?*" She looked skeptically at her phone. "I want the *police* to find him."

"The police can't do anything until after forty-eight hours. Do you have a recent photo of him?"

She went into the bedroom, came back with a

snapshot of a balding old man in a Hawaiian shirt. "Last summer, at the Seniors Dance." She shook her head. "*Aiyah*. The old fool."

"You'll need some tape." She started crying, came back with some loose Band-Aids.

"Please help me find him, *Ah Sir*."

IT TOOK NINETY minutes for Ah Fook's Photo to attach a blowup of the old man's picture to Jack's handwritten MISSING PERSON heading with the wife's phone number and print thirty-six posters for shop fronts and lampposts in the area. He hoped she'd get a call in Chinese, because she wouldn't know how to handle a call in English.

The sky turned dark while he waited, polishing off a plate of *hom gnow faahn* at Half-Ass on Pell.

Ah Fook had tossed in a roll of tape gratis. *Community service*, he'd called it. Jack posted several alerts around the Seniors Center, some fliers in the old man's Hester Street neighborhood, two near the Fifth Precinct for the cops and local auxiliaries.

He gave the old woman the remainder of the stack of posters and the roll of tape, along with his detective's card.

She thanked him and offered him tea. He politely declined, imagining instead a shot of XO or Johnny Walker. They'd have to wait forty-eight hours, but he knew people with poor mental health often wound up in the East River before then.

He left the Hester Street tenement, and after thirteen hours on the job, decided to head home to Sunset Park. He caught a minibus back to Brooklyn.

On Eighth Avenue he bought a fresh six-pack of Heineken at the 24 Deli, and a new bottle of XO from Wah Fu Liquors. The night had cooled, and on the three-block walk home he imagined a hot shower followed by a cold brew.

THE HOT SHOWER sucked the stress out of his muscles but didn't dissolve the mess in his mind. *That* was what the boilermakers were for, he knew. He'd started the day out looking for a *person of interest* in an assault case no one admits happened, and ended it looking for a Missing Person who no longer remembers who he is.

The first frosty gulps settled him, and he noticed a message on his phone that had arrived while he showered. An unfamiliar number, something he'd expected from Alexandra, keeping him posted, like she'd promised.

Hearing due soon. You may need to speak to Judge.

It wasn't the message he wanted but he was glad for the connection. He wanted to call her back but knew he'd promised not to. *She was just protecting the kid and the custody deal.*

He wanted to say *I miss you. Miss the touch of your hand. The taste of your lips. The smell of flowers in your hair. The scent of you after.*

The message had given him a heart rush that he needed to slow down. He wanted to reach out and touch the memories but couldn't, reaching instead for the XO and another Heineken.

Thinking of the missing Alzheimer's *lo gung*, he wondered if people still stayed together, losing themselves in each other, until they no longer even recognize who they are.

He downed half the mug, switched off the lights. Closed his eyes. The questions and contradictions brought him back around to:

Her long black hair. Her runner's legs.

The pretty face belonged to May McCann. He remembered her question.

Is there anyone you can turn to?

He took a deep *shaolin* breath, heard himself answering out loud.

"No. There's no one."

He drained the mug, closed his eyes to darkness and waited for the swirl of surrender.

Red Lobster

JOJO KNEW THE area and picked the Red Lobster in Valley Stream. It had a big parking lot and was used to serving groups of foreign tourists. Lucky's new crew would be forgotten soon after their plates hit the table. More important, the location kept them off the NYPD radar. Long Island cops had their own routines and protocols.

Jojo knew about how places like the Temple Garden Spa operated. Friday and Saturday nights were the busiest. The tally and cash-out for the weekend usually took place on Sunday night, when the triad managers and *dailos* skimmed off and divvied up the proceeds before anything passed down through the ranks. Payday on the streets was Monday morning.

Hit the Spa in the wee hours early Sunday morning was the plan. An easy rip-off, on the face of it, robbing a pimp-and-pussy operation. Jojo knew some of the whores and *gai wong* pimps there. Everyone there looking to fuck but not to fight, especially against masked men with guns. Working girls were there to earn, not to get deported. *Nobody* wants a piece of a violent rip-off crew, knowing it was best to just disappear and let the alpha dogs settle matters.

They'd engage any Ghost crew that happened by, with both Lam brothers armed with the Uzi and the shotgun.

They arrived separately, within minutes of each other. Lucky in the Buick, Loo Ga in his Mazda. Say Low parked his Charger at the far end, across from the Lam brothers in their utility Suburban. Jojo and Jadine waited in a generic minivan. All the vehicles had tinted windows. Cowboy was the last to arrive, popping out of a *see gay* car-service sedan.

Once they were inside and seated, Lucky watched his Lucky Eight bond over the surf 'n' turf and cocktails. He waited until the waitresses left before breaking down the plan.

"Cowboy," he said, "you go in first, check it out. It should be busy, so ask for an hour on the table. Call me on the setup. Wait ten minutes, then ask for a half hour on the doughnut chair instead."

Jojo and Jadine sipped their drinks, two grifters awaiting their marching orders.

"Loo Ga, you're the lead. Go in with Jojo." Both men nodded at each other. "I'll be right behind you. Get the *gai wongs* and the manager to one side. They control the money." Loo Ga grinned, drained his vodka. Jojo sneered contemptuously, imagining the pimps he was going to get his revenge on. Jadine was quiet, knew her place.

"Lam brothers, you follow us in, push all the hos and johns into the basement. Some of them may be butt naked, but make sure no one has a cell phone." The Lam brothers nodded, chewing on their lobster tails.

"You're the last ones out," Lucky continued, stone cold. "Make sure you have that quart of gasoline. Send everyone a message." He turned his attention to Say Low.

"Say Low will be waiting in the van. Around the corner." Say Low raised his drink like a toast, drained it.

"Jadine, you're the backup. Minivan, a block away. If all goes well, we won't need you. Meet us back at College Point." The Lam brothers had a garage there.

"Everyone clear on all this?" Lucky laughed at the murmurs of acknowledgment.

"Another round!" he called in the direction of the waitresses. *The game has begun,* he thought, *and it won't be over until I get back to Chinatown.*

Death Do Us Part

THE CALL CAME in at 5 A.M., a dispatcher's voice cutting through the foggy static in his head.

"You got a body. MEs at the scene."

"What's *the twenty?*" was all he could manage.

"Fifty-four Bayard." *Chinatown* calling again.

"Fifth Precinct." Another detail he already knew.

"Five-four Bayard. Copy that."

THE SIX-STORY TENEMENT walk-up at 54 Bayard was worse than the one he'd grown up in on Pell Street. These apartments shared a closet toilet in the exterior hallway, a frozen seat on the crapper in the winter, a stinking sticky seat in the summer.

The female uniform on post, what some of the older cops called *a skirt*, was waiting on the top floor. She looked white Irish and wasn't wearing a skirt, and had a chiseled face and regulation-smart head to boot.

"Detective Yu?" she asked.

"Yeah," he flashed his shield. "What have you got?"

"Sixty-one-year-old female," her jargon precise. "*Asian.* Collapsed while ironing her clothes."

"*Ironing* before five A.M.?"

"Husband called 911. EMS pronounced her dead twenty minutes ago. We're waiting on the ME pickup." She stared at him like he was the first Asian cop she'd ever seen, who outranked her but in her eyes there was something less. He'd seen it before, tried not to take offense.

Female officers faced sexism all along the chain of command, the notion that women weren't up to the job. He knew, because he'd trained Alexandra to shoot, that a woman with a gun could be just as capable as a man. Sometimes *more* capable.

But at least she didn't say meat wagon, he thought.

"Okay," as he digested her information, "thanks for the cliff-notes version. Husband inside?" He met her stare.

She nodded. "He's probably in shock." He pushed the door, went past her.

THE OLD CHINESE man had to be over seventy years old, reminded Jack of his own *Pa*. From the last big wave of Cantonese stock, the old man sat on a milk crate, in a quiet solemn grieving more of words and gestures than tears.

He seemed to be talking to himself.

"She was getting her clothes ready. She takes the early train to Long Island, and has to rush in the morning."

The room was a hoarder's nightmare. Stacks of news-papers, mail-order goods, blocking off entire sections of the apartment. Pots and buckets placed strategically beneath the leaky ceiling. Candles arranged haphazardly throughout.

On a wall shelf were some photos, colorful ones of

them together at a senior center, and old sepia-toned pictures of his army days from World War II.

The woman lay face up on the linoleum floor. The EMS techs had turned her over and tried to no avail to resuscitate her.

She looked finally at peace.

The husband shifted on the crate he'd placed next to her, the two of them framed in the yellow light of the lone bulb hanging down from the leaky ceiling.

"She was just trying to get ready for work," he mumbled.

"*Ah sook*," Jack consoled the senior. "*Uncle*, we have to honor her. Honor the lifetime of memories."

The man nodded, accepting the wisdom from the young cop's mouth.

"In this country," he said, "you work until you die."

Jack looked around at the stacks of boxes and shopping bags full of Chinatown junk. He wondered how the old couple had come to this.

"She died getting ready for work."

Jack turned his attention from the sad scene when the female cop poked her head inside the door.

"Wagon's here," she announced quietly, near the end of her one-off dose of overtime in the Fifth Precinct.

He turned back to the old man.

"You may want to pick out a nice dress," he suggested.

"Dress?"

"Something you'd want to remember her by. Like something she'd wear on vacation."

"*Vacation?* Yes, she needed a vacation."

"Sunny skies." He forced a sad smile.

"Sunny skies," the old man repeated as the morgue attendants loaded his wife onto the gurney.

"You don't have to go to the morgue. You know the Wah Fook funeral parlor on Mulberry Street?"

"Everyone in Chinatown knows Wah Fook."

"I'll ask the medical examiner to make the transfer when they're done."

The man frowned and nodded his agreement as Jack followed the body out, pulling the door shut behind him.

He watched from the sidewalk as the black morgue wagon pulled off the curb and headed into the daylight leaking over the Lower East Side. Death was never pretty, he knew, but at least this was a natural death, not a homicide, as far as he could see. The poor woman worked until she dropped dead. She'd *killed* herself, in essence.

Did that make him care less? Pa had worked himself sick as well. Still, he was saddened, but without the added anger. He felt out of sync. At 6 A.M. in Chinatown, it was too early to call the Wah Fook parlor, too early even for Eddie's Coffee Shop or the Tofu King. *Everything closed, Chinatown a ghost town.* And he wasn't in the right mind or mood to bang out a report with the dregs of the overnight shift at the Fifth.

As he walked the deserted streets away from Mott, he heard May McCann's, *Doctor McCann's,* voice in his head.

"So you're *disaffected emotionally*, detective?"

"I never *said* that," he remembered answering.

At 6 A.M., even the whores are turning for home.

He changed course toward Tribeca and the all-night-diner hope of an early-bird breakfast special.

HE REPORTED TO the day shift at the Fifth Precinct, typing the death report on a table in the back of the station house, where the detectives filed their cases. The old woman had succumbed to a heart attack, a *natural* death, so the paperwork was minimal, cut and dried.

The deceased was Mrs. Chun Yook Ha, age 61. She resided at 54 Bayard, Apartment 5B. EMS pronounced her dead and the morgue would classify the COD, or "cause of death," as cardiac arrest and mark the time around 0530 hours. Five-thirty in the morning.

Once they released the body, the Wah Fook funeral parlor would take care of the rest. Jack needed to make sure the widowed husband, Kitman *James* Chun, followed up. Most Chinatown Chinese didn't have much of a nest egg but pragmatically would have their burial insurance paid up.

He was hoping to catch a few minutes with CO Captain Marino but he hadn't yet appeared.

Jack left the report in the captain's tray.

WHEN HE GOT around to the Wah Fook parlor, the manager confirmed that Mr. Chun had indeed stopped by and signed off on the funeral package. Jack thanked the funeral director for his help and was on the way out when his cell phone jangled again.

"Ah *Sir?*"

Every time he'd heard the Chinese slang for *cop* it'd been followed by trouble. He took a small *shaolin* breath.

It was the old Toishanese woman who'd lost track of her equally old Alzheimer's husband. He heard new life in her voice.

"They found *lo-gung* and he is resting now!"

"Where?" Jack asked.

"In Columbus Park."

"He was okay?"

"He was feeding the pigeons."

"The pigeons?"

"People said he was tossing them bits of two *cha siew baos* he had in a bag."

"Where's he now?"

"I had him checked at the Health Clinic but he's home with me now. Strange, though."

"*Strange?* How so?"

"When they asked him where he'd been, he said he visited his old buddies at the American Legion, on Canal Street. But nobody there remembered him. He did serve in World War II but wasn't a member of the Kimlau Post."

Jack momentarily pondered the mysteries of the mind.

"When I picked him up, you know the first thing he asked?"

"What?"

"What's for lunch?"

Jack couldn't help laughing.

"Like he never left."

"Good," said Jack, relieved. "Please, *ah por*, keep an eye on him now."

"Yes. And I have something to give you. A small token."

"Not necessary, ah por."

"Yes, I will call you . . ."

"*M'sai*," Jack cut her off, before hanging up. *Not necessary*. He'd promised Pa, as a cop, he'd never take anything while on the job, especially from Chinese.

A case that ended happily made him feel positive, better than how the brutal cases depressed him. Good karma flowed, and the rest of the shift was peaceful. For the time being, nobody killed anybody in Manhattan South.

Pussy Time

THE TEMPLE GARDEN Spa, No. 2600, was at the far end of the commercial strip on Thirty-Seventh Avenue, leading to and from LaGuardia Airport. The offices and small businesses at that end were closed after dark, and the Temple Spa was a destination point rather than a tourist discovery.

Cowboy wore a fuddy-duddy shirt with black slacks and sneakers, looking like Chinese-restaurant kitchen help out for some late-night excitement. He was used to the play *johns* gave to surveillance cameras, an *I'm harmless jes wanna fuck* vibe. Easy enough, they buzzed him in, just another *hom sup low*.

"One hour," he said to the Chinese lady behind the counter. "On the table."

There was a video monitor there that she glanced at occasionally. *He'd need to get the videotape, especially since he was the only one of the crew not to wear a mask.* She handed him a small card with a number on it.

"It may be fifteen minutes," she said, motioning to a set of lounge chairs and padded benches where two men sat in dim light watching a TV screen.

He heard low-key music floating in the air.

"Sure," he answered, taking a seat on one of the benches behind the men. They were both enjoying their drinks, and Cowboy figured they wouldn't notice the slight bulge of his ankle holster and the flat little .22-caliber Colt nestled there.

There was a tray table with plastic bottles of tea and water. He chose water and took a swallow. He could hear soft groans from the little stalls lined up against the wall behind the Chinese-style curtains.

After a few minutes, a satisfied customer came out from one of the back stalls and paid the woman at the counter. *She put the cash somewhere beneath the counter.* The satiated john departed, and Cowboy knew the crew would spot him and wait until he cleared the street before they approached. He took another sip of water and scanned the scene.

There was just the one guy at the door, an old-school geezer too old not to be armed. He'd probably earned the post and couldn't be underestimated. The two men watching TV could be customers, a manager and pimp, or just backup. He couldn't tell which, and since neither man spoke, he couldn't venture a guess.

He put down the water bottle, watched to see if either of the men headed for the back stalls. He didn't see any numbered cards in their hands. *Or maybe there were a few minutes of rest between shifts for the working girls?*

If it *was* his turn, Cowboy knew to ask for fifteen minutes in the doughnut chair instead. He knew, in the closing hour among the last dregs of the night crawlers, a short stint at the doughnut chair was a good deal for any massage girl. *Better than having to polish off the knobs of the last hom sup lows.* Also, the chair provided him an excuse not to be undressed, ready for action.

Another minute passed. Neither man moved, and Cowboy made the call as planned. He punched in the number 1 and then 2: 1 for *one man at door,* 2 for *two men waiting.* He knew Lucky and the others would get the picture.

He resisted the urge to touch his ankle holster.

THE STREET WAS deserted.

The five men slipping out of the dark van appeared to have attended a celebration, with the party now drifting toward the Temple Spa around the corner.

Cowboy went to the counter and requested the doughnut chair instead, just so he could get an eyeball on the monitor or videotape deck.

The counter lady was watching the screen with a curious expression as the group of men approached. *Something odd about them. Their faces like cartoon masks.* She caught her breath as one of them suddenly reached up and sprayed a cloud that blacked out the camera view.

Cowboy stepped from the counter and toward the front as the buzzer sounded. The two seated men glanced toward the door. The old door guard kept his right hand near his hip, took a gander through the peephole. *Looked like a bachelor party something.* Usually, he'd get the nod of approval from the counter.

He turned just in time to see the blur of Cowboy's fist before hearing the sound of his own nose breaking. The immediate white whipflashes and the rush of blood dropped him to the grimy floor like a sack of rice.

The other two men rose from their seats but were frozen in place as Cowboy opened the door for Loo Ga and Jojo, bursting in with guns drawn. Lucky stormed in behind them and they pushed the two men back, behind the counter.

Cowboy took a bowie knife from the old man's waistband, still in its sheath, as the Lam brothers barreled in.

"Look under the counter!" he yelled at Loo Ga before booting the sniveling old man into a corner.

Men in Halloween masks talking it up in Cantonese.

The Lam brothers toted two semiauto pistols and a shotgun. They began herding the half-naked customers and working girls toward the back of the spa, people who didn't want to argue with a shotgun. Short Lam took their cell phones and wallets.

Cowboy covered the scene with his deadly little Colt.

Jojo took a switchblade off the younger of the two men, the one he knew was the pimp *gai wong* of the rub joint. Lucky watched as Jojo bitch-slapped him, with Loo Ga slamming him from behind. The other man shuddered, fearing *his*.

"*Lun yeung!* Where's the cash?" Loo Ga demanded. Jojo clicked open the switchblade.

"I don't know!" the man pleaded. "I just supply the girls." Jojo bitch-slapped him again.

"You call those hags *girls*? *Kai daai!*"

Lucky watched as Loo Ga put his Luger to the head of the older man, saying:

"Open the safe."

"I don't know . . ." as Loo Ga clocked him across the ear with the butt of the pistol.

"Ayeeowwww!"

The counter lady looked ready to panic but Cowboy calmed her.

"No one needs to get hurt. Just point to the safe, and pull the videotape out."

Trembling, she did as she was told. Cowboy pocketed the videotape.

Lucky grinned behind his Popeye mask as Cowboy moved the lady to the Lam brothers.

Jojo handcuffed the pimp and kept the switchblade against his quivering face as the other man was made to kneel in front of a hotel-type safe. Loo Ga pressed the gun barrel against his temple.

"This worth dying for?" Lucky asked him. "Got a girl-friend? Wife? Kids?"

"Yes!"

"Want to see them again?"

"Yes! Please . . ."

"Then open the safe. No one gets hurt. Tomorrow, business as usual."

"Who *are* you guys?" Loo Ga smacked him again.

"Ayyeooow!"

"Open the fuckin' safe!"

Jojo dragged the point of the switchblade across the pimp's cheek, drawing a line of blood.

"*Hoyla! Hoy la!*" the pimp hollered. "Open the safe!"

The man punched in a security code and opened the strongbox before they shoved him aside. Jojo scooped out wads of cash, credit cards, and assorted pharmaceuticals. Lucky signaled the others.

They'd been there almost ten minutes and needed to roll. Cowboy notified Say Low and Jadine, sending them a prearranged "0" over the phone. *Fire up your engines, ready to roll.*

Lucky led the way out as Loo Ga and Jojo followed with the sack of loot. Cowboy signaled the Lams, waited a few seconds before trailing the others to the van.

The Lam brothers closed it out, splashing a quart of gasoline around the doorway. They torched it. The workers and johns would have to exit through the back of the house, and there would be no pursuit.

The Lams were the last ones, piling in and sliding the van door shut as Say Low drove them calmly toward the highway lights of the LIE and the brothers' garage.

THE LAMS HAD a big garage, a makeshift aluminum shack next to their home, large enough to park their old Suburban and a second, smaller car. Tonight the Suburban was parked on the street.

Their house was at the end of an urban cul-de-sac, the street ending on their block and then splitting two ways through neighborhoods curling back toward the highway. They'd erected the shack garage themselves, using military guidelines.

Loo Ga had parked his Mazda nearby, prepared to drive

Lucky back to Flushing. Say Low left his Charger a block away from the Mazda, ready to give Cowboy a lift to Manhattan. Jadine arrived last, parked across from the house, and waited for Jojo.

Say Low rolled the van in easily, everyone breathing sighs of relief when he cut the engine. The Lams secured the garage doors and they gathered around a workbench as Lucky emptied the loot bag. He heard murmurs and grunts as they saw the pile in the cone of lamplight. *Bundles of cash from the safe, from the wallets, a dozen credit cards, plastic ziplock bags of different colored pills.*

The Lams never took any money from the massage ladies after they pleaded for it, cried over how they'd *earned* it. They also didn't snatch the gold chains or rings off the johns but did keep their wallets and cell phones.

Lucky split the safe cash off for Loo Ga to count. He emptied the cash and credit cards from the wallets, separated them. *Eight hundred cash, four credit cards.* He added the wallet cards to the bogus credit cards from the safe. He put the wallets aside, empty except for family photos of wife and kids, for Loo Ga. Loo would find ways to blackmail the johns, by threatening to send pics to the wifey or to the job.

"Twenty-four thousand and eight hundred," announced Loo Ga.

Lucky tossed the credit cards to Jojo. "Better put these to work quick," he instructed, knowing Jojo and Jadine would rack up fake charges at the shady massage, porn, and entertainment businesses that the Taiwanese Big Circle operated in Flushing.

"We'll square up later," Lucky said as Jojo hustled with the credit cards to Jadine waiting in the car. The cards would buck up Jadine's half-share for just driving around this time. Some extra cash as a bonus would keep them both happy.

The bags of pills, mostly ecstasy, with ludes and amphetamines thrown in, he valued at a couple of thousand dollars, tops. He tossed them to the Lam brothers. *Who in this crew knew how to move pharmaceuticals better than them?* The pills would goose their lesser shares.

"*Dailo* gets a quarter," said Loo Ga, parsing six thousand aside for Lucky. "And as agreed, the shares." He kept four thousand for himself, the same he gave to Lucky to hold for Jojo. He gave three thousand to Cowboy, two thousand each to the Lam brothers, and to Say Low.

Before Say Low left with Cowboy, Lucky gave them another thousand each from his own share. *Is everybody happy?* Loo Ga stood quietly impressed by how Lucky treated the crew fairly.

They were the last to leave the Lams' garage, both men quiet on the drive to Flushing. Lucky didn't mind paying out of his share this time. It showed solidarity with the crew, and generosity on his part. *A happy crew was a productive crew.* More Art of War. Besides, money wasn't *all* that he was after. He wanted *power*. He wanted back on Mott Street and knew the money would follow.

A few thousand to bond the crew? It was a cheap price to pay.

*　*　*

LUCKY TOLD LOO Ga to drop him off on Main Street, three blocks from the Asia Manor. He didn't want any of the crew to know where he was staying. *Better for everyone and less chance of betrayal.* Dawn still hadn't wiped the after-hours from the sky as Loo Ga pulled the Mazda to the curb.

"That's it, boss?"

"Yeah, for a few days," answered Lucky. "Why, you impatient?"

"Nah."

"So enjoy your cash a little."

"Yeah, will do."

"We go again next week."

"Awwright." Loo Ga grinned as Lucky climbed out of the Mazda. "I'll be ready, *but . . .*"

"But *what?*"

"No *jerkoffs*, okay?"

Lucky laughed as Loo Ga drove away. *No jerkoffs.* He smirked. *So far so good.*

LATER, HE SAT shirtless in the luxe armchair, in the cool quiet dark of the Asia Manor studio. He fired up some sinsemilla, looking out the picture window at the sparkling points of light in the Main Street distance. The view inspired vivid brass and neon memories from his heart of Chinatown.

Timing is everything, he knew, but wondered how much time he had left in this second life. All the Chinatown *dailos* knew:

Patience is a virtue.

But too much will hurt you, echoed the boyz on the street. Not so much Sun Tzu but world-wise gang-boy wisdom.

The sinsemilla burned an umami sickly sweet.

And he was lucky so far. He laughed out loud. *But he'd been Lucky forever, even granted a second life!*

They'd robbed Charley Joe, and the Temple Spa, without a shot being fired, just old-fashioned thuggery and terror; a couple of pistol-whippings and broken noses, and Jojo went and cut a pimp, but nothing fatal or life-threatening.

And *flaming* the place was Jojo's idea, a bit of revenge that would also send a message. *Payback for stealing his massage parlor.* No one expected the FDNY though. *What kind of fire can you start with a quart of gasoline anyway?*

He figured the manager crew would put it out quickly, but those panicked idiots let it get out of hand. If the Temple Spa hadn't been at the far end of the strip, and if there had been any structural damage, the takedown raid might have gotten more unwanted interest.

He toked down the weed, wanted to believe it wouldn't turn out to be a problem.

In the distance, the bright lights continued to call. The new crew was happy for the time being, but he turned his attention to the next job, a shout in the face of the Ghost Legion. He'd let the crew leaders, Loo Ga and Jojo, know soon enough.

Soon enough, he'd put the On Yee on notice.

No Problem

HER WORDS CAME in a message on his phone. Judge ruled out the videotape. You're clear. Alexandra clearing one hurdle for him. He wanted to message her back but knew it'd go to some dead end somewhere.

No problem, he texted back anyway. See you soon.

He didn't feel optimistic.

The phone jangled again, trembling in his hand. He hoped it was Alexandra. "Detective Yu?" A man's voice, with a law enforcement edge.

"Correct." Like answering a challenge.

"McAuliffe, from the One-Ten."

Jack scratched his mind for a few seconds.

"You the duty sarge?"

"That's right. You were looking for Chinese angles in CompStat, right? About a week ago?"

"That's right. Why? What's up?"

"Last night there was a fire. A *Chi-nees* massage parlor on Thirty-Seventh Avenue. Called the Temple Garden."

Jack held his tongue, wondering if any of it led to Jojo.

"FDNY and EMS responded. As did one of the sector cars that caught the call."

"Go on," Jack prodded, the word *Chinese* sticking in his brain.

"It wasn't much of a fire. They issued a citation. EMS handled two injuries, both male. One Chinaman with a broken nose and a hernia. Said he tripped and fell on his face." *Chinaman* also stuck in his forehead.

"The other . . . guy?"

"Claimed to be a customer. Had a cut on his face. He also tripped and fell."

"Whoa, what're they serving there?" Jack quipped. "*Anyone else* trip and fall?" *Either his people were exceptionally clumsy or they avoided involvement with the authorities.*

"Haha. Their English was sketchy, so something might have gotten lost in translation. Know what I'm sayin'?"

"No massage girls, or other customers?"

"Negative. Must've run off after the fire started. Like a Chinese fire drill." *Running the gamut of Chinaman jokes.*

He tried to guess where the deal was leading but was missing a few cards. He decided to take the Mustang out to Queens again.

Temple Garden.

"Anything else?" Jack asked.

"Nope, that's it. TPO's on file."

"Great. Thanks a lot, McAuliffe."

"You *got* it! One question, though."

"Shoot."

"Where's a good place to eat in Chinatown?"

* * *

BEFORE HEADING TO the garage at Confucius, he decided to visit *The United National* to see if its editor, Vincent Chin, had heard anything. Vincent had unofficially assisted Jack on previous cases.

The National, Luen Hop Kwok, was Chinatown's oldest Chinese-language daily and was Pa's favorite hometown newspaper. The storefront office was across from the Men's Mission on White Street.

He arrived empty-handed, neglecting to bring Vincent a customary takeout cup of *nai cha* tea.

"Hey, Yu!" greeted Vincent, looking up from a page layout. The printed Chinese characters were still typeset by hand.

"Hey, Chin," answered Jack.

"What brings you down?"

"There was a fire last night. In Queens. Was wondering if you covered it."

"Was it in Elmhurst?"

"Yes. How'd you know that?"

"One of our junior stringers covers the emergency blotter in Queens."

"And?"

"It came in too late for today's run. We were lining it up for tomorrow's edition, along with a piece on diversity, or lack of it, in the FDNY." He made a few keystrokes and the news article appeared on his desktop screen, in Chinese.

Vincent translated.

"The Temple Garden Spa and Massage. A small fire.

FDNY put it out within minutes, with just handheld fire extinguishers. Some carpeting, a couch, and window drapes were damaged. A worker claimed the fire started after-hours, caused by a careless smoker whose cigarette fell out of an ashtray. The fire lieutenant noted the smell of gasoline and termed the blaze *suspicious*. They were issued a fine for not having a working extinguisher at a business premises. Then a paragraph on fire-code regulations."

"Anything on EMS?"

"Hold on. He wrote it as a *fire* piece." Jack waited as Vincent scrolled to the end of the article.

"Okay, *here*. One man they took to Elmhurst General. A broken nose. There was a second man. Had a cut on his face. DMT. Declined medical treatment. No names."

"Thanks, brother," Jack said. "I owe you a *nai cha*."

Vincent chuckled as Jack left the storefront.

HE FIRED UP the Mustang, and rolling against the flow of afternoon traffic into Manhattan made it from Confucius Towers to Elmhurst in twenty-three minutes.

He badged the supervisor at Elmhurst General and requested the overnight logs.

"What time was this?" she asked.

"I'd guess two-thirty to three-thirty A.M."

"There was only one admittance around then." She showed Jack his outpatient Medicaid information. *Woo Sik Kee. Sixty-seven years old*. They'd billed for *Septum damage cartilage. Wheelchair, crutches for hernia*. His photo a Chinese bulldog face. A Chinatown OG with a Mott

Street address, *188 Mott*. Just off Hester Street. Jack knew those streets well, at the edge of the urban playground that was Chinatown.

"He left two hours ago. Someone picked him up."

"Name? Sign-in sheet?"

"Right *here*." She traced her finger to an entry.

"Dewey Lai."

Jack knew *dew lai* was shorthand Cantonese slang for *fuck you*. The broken nose was a triad wise guy, like whoever picked him up. The gang's little joke. He thanked the supervisor for her help.

There may not have been a crime committed, but he knew that the *Luen Hop Kwok* maintained a decades-long Chinatown crime file, and to one of the old-timer reporters, the name Woo Sik Kee might ring a bell.

He called Vincent Chin before weaving through heavy traffic back into Manhattan. The return trip took almost an hour's worth of *shaolin* patience.

BY THE TIME he got to *The National*'s storefront, Vincent had the answers. Jack handed him the takeout cup of *nai cha* before he began.

"Woo Sik Kee is a longtime member of the Wo Lok, a triad. The Wo Group is a Cantonese subset, dating back to the eighteenth century. Now it's just thirteen organizations, representing almost everything that's got a *Wo* in its name: restaurants and coffee shops, bakeries, dry goods, produce supply and warehousing, gift shops, and, apparently, massage parlors."

"Something extra, to relieve the stress, I guess," Jack said.

"The Wo Lok, which has a dark history of murder and robbery in Hong Kong, was once the most powerful crime group there in the 1950s. But lots of infighting now."

"How about our *Uncle Woo?*"

"Woo Sik Kee is a Wo old-timer. Used to be known on the street as 'Whiskee' because he drank Johnny Walker. Suspect in a fatal gang assault but got dismissed after the others fled. This was the 1970s. How old is he now?"

"Sixty-eight, according to Medicaid."

"An ex hatchet man?"

"The Wo, with all their rackets. Drug trafficking, prostitution. Gambling, extortion, money laundering. Whiskee was probably an enforcer once."

An old martial artist? Jack considered. Or just another clumsy Chinese *slip and fall* like Dup Choy?

He went to the Fifth Precinct and checked the desktop database. There were no records of crimes dating back more than a few years. Most of the crimes from the old days, including cold cases, had been manually logged, then copied and stored on microfilm. Little had been transferred to computer files. Most lay buried in the records dungeons of the NYPD.

Captain Marino's office was empty, and he decided to head north, through the neighborhood.

One eighty-eight Mott Street. Apartment 2A, right above the Long Kee Grocery. Noisy in the daytime, dead quiet at night with all the businesses shut down. The lock on the street door was already broken and he went straight up to 2A. He rapped firmly on the door and called out.

"Woo *sook*! Open up, Uncle! *Chaai yun! Real* police!"

There was dead silence for a minute and he rapped again, louder this time.

"Open up or I'll report you to Social Security!" He heard a slight rustling sound, then footsteps inside.

"You go to jail, you'll lose your Medicaid too!" He kicked the bottom of the door.

"Last chance!"

Slowly, he heard the bolt slide back, the chain latch rattle, then the turn of the knob. The door opened a crack and he could see a man's face with a bandaged nose.

"*Wan ngo ah?*" Jack challenged. "You fucking with me?"

"No, Ah Sir." Showing wary respect now. An old nasally voice, full of remorse or cunning.

"You work for the Temple Garden?"

"Not really."

"Not *really*. You mean they pay you off the books?"

The old-school gangster was silent.

"If I report you to the IRS, Uncle, especially with your tong connections, you'll lose your Social Security benefits, and your Medicaid, too. You *know* that, right?" Jack bluffed.

"Please, Ah Sir . . ."

"*If* I report you. So you do work at the whorehouse."

"*Massage* house only, Ah Sir."

"Yeah, right. Better tell me what happened. How'd you get the busted nose? And don't tell me you fell down." The man hesitated, then thought better of lying to the *jouh gow* running-dog Chinese cop.

"We got robbed. Men in masks. I got sucker punched."

"How many men?"

"Four or five. Maybe six."

"Which is it? Four or six?"

"I couldn't tell. I saw stars, I couldn't breathe, and the blood . . ."

"They spoke English?"

"They spoke Chinese."

"What kind of Chinese?"

"What *kind*?"

"Toishanese. Mandarin. What?"

"Cantonese."

"Like Hong Kong Cantonese?"

"You could say that."

"Who owns the place?"

"Who?"

"Your *boss*, wiseguy."

"I don't know who owns it. That's above me."

"Who pays you?"

Woo hesitated, and Jack pressed the OG.

"I'll report you to the *gwai los* right fuckin' now, and you'll lose everything. You'll be lucky not to go to jail or be deported. You understand me, *kai dai*?"

"I get a *stipend* from the Wo."

"You're a triad member."

"Yes."

The Wo group led to the On Yee Association.

"Your friend got his face cut."

"*Not* my friend."

"A customer?"

"He's the *gai wong*, pimp. They'll be back in business as soon as they air it out."

"A Wo pimp? Better not lie to me."

"No lie."

"I know where you live now."

Woo nodded silently.

"I can fuck with you anytime. Or I can send *gwai lo* cops."

Woo frowned.

"No lie."

"Because you know, I'll be back."

"Please, no lie."

Jack let him go, too small a catch to keep, but maybe more valuable as a snitch one day. He slipped his detective's card through the crack in the doorway, saw it fall to the floor.

"*Remember* me, Uncle," he warned. But he was already thinking about Lucky and Jojo as he stepped down the tenement building and wondered whether they'd had anything to do with the Temple Garden or if things were starting to heat up in Chinatown like every time the weather changed.

Cantonese

BEFORE THE SINSEMILLA chilled Lucky unconscious, the thoughts already took hold. The Canton Group had operated eight restaurants, from takeout joints to sit-downs with waiter service, throughout the city, meaning Manhattan, Queens, and Brooklyn. The investors were *foreign* capital, partnered with local money, in many cases for visa purposes. In many cases wealthy Asians sent their grandchildren to schools in NYC and bought condos as investments in the process.

He saw the Cantons were paying almost a hundred thousand a year in protection and he needed to press them further. He could do that only through a significant event, where they got scared that it could hamper their money operations, likely to bring the cops and the *federal* down.

He was dreaming something about *an old wives' tale* when he woke up, strangely feeling the need to call Loo Ga.

Wife Swap

LUCKY WANTED TO make sure he had the story right.

"Tell me again," he said to Loo Ga. "About the Chow cousins."

They'd agreed to meet at a hilltop café in Long Island City, a sunny outdoor spot that overlooked the East River. At midafternoon the place was near empty and Lucky knew that two Chinese drinking beers weren't going to require much service.

The indifferent waiter brought them two mugs of draft and left them alone. Their view included the Williamsburg Bridge far to the left, the Silvercup factory sign closer by. Across the river they saw lower Manhattan, and the top twenty stories of Confucius Towers.

Confucius Towers was Lucky's Chinatown beacon, on street level just a block away from Mott Street, calling him home.

They touched mugs, took a swallow each before Loo Ga began the tale he'd heard from *dai gor* Kid Taiwan in friendlier days.

"The Chow cousins, Richie and Ronnie, what a pair of hard-ons. *Jerkoffs*. Their families partnered up on the restaurants and put them in charge. Richie at the Canton Palace. Ronnie at the Canton Gourmet. So, the two jerkoffs didn't trust each other, right? So they swapped wives and . . ."

"Swapped wives?"

"That's how the joke went. Richie put his wife as head cashier at the Gourmet, and Ronnie put *his* wife likewise at the Palace. *That* way, their wives watched the money, and could help cook the second set of books while spying on the workers."

"Keeping everything and *everyone* in line," Lucky said.

"Exactly."

"When did Taiwan tell you this?"

"Coulda been over Christmas, New Year's."

They were quiet a moment, both taking the chance to down another gulp of beer.

"Five months ago."

"Yeah, *before* you got shot."

He liked the story, figured if *the way to a man's heart is through his stomach*, then the way to his cash was through his woman, through *lo por*, the *wifey* . . .

The sunlight shimmered on the river, glinted off the high-rise windows of Confucius Towers like long-distance flashbulbs.

Everything calling him back and the raid was already forming in his head.

Three men and a getaway driver at each location. Before closing time. Come in cool, it'll look like family or community. Disguise the strong-arm. Deception is everything. Use the big menus. Make it like you're ordering the last big takeout of the night.

They drained their beers, left the absent waiter some table money.

"Let's go," Lucky said.

Loo Ga followed him, eager for the next score.

THE PALACE AND the Gourmet were three miles apart, from Jackson Heights to Rego Park. A mile and a half as the crow flies. Seven minutes by car. They closed at eleven on weekend nights, cashing in on late dinners, takeout orders, and the early club crowd.

Eleven P.M. was also the hour that patrol cops started leaning for home, toward the end of another shift in the inner city, Lucky knew. He waited in the Regal with the Lam brothers while Say Low went down the block to see if the Gourmet was empty. He patted the nine-millimeter Taurus on his hip, choosing it over the Beretta, a much cheaper throwaway if necessary. He'd assigned the sawed-off Mossberg to Tall Lam, but both brothers also carried military sidearms, hefty Browning .45s. Per the brothers' suggestion, Lucky planned the raid on military precision, a ten-minute hit-and-run.

He checked his watch and imagined Jadine checking out the Palace while Jojo, Loo Ga, and Cowboy waited in their *borrowed* SUV. The street was now dark and sparsely traveled.

A signal from Say Low was all they needed.

* * *

ACROSS FROM THE Palace, Jadine saw two customers inside, turned and raised both arms for Loo Ga watching her from the SUV. Jojo and Cowboy were armed and ready.

Loo Ga's phone buzzed out Lucky's bold text command in the green window: GO. He tapped his Luger as the others coolly followed him out.

THE THREE CASUALLY dressed men walked a few lengths apart, led by Lucky, passing Say Low returning to the Regal. Lucky knew Say Low would fire the car up, letting it idle while keeping the headlights off.

The Regal was already pointed toward the highway.

Three diners exited as Lucky entered, activating the alarm timer on his watch: 10:30 P.M. The Lams lagged behind to avoid the last diners, who decided to cross the street.

In the empty dining room, there was a man in a black suit standing beside a pretty lady at the cashier's counter. *Ronnie Chow*, Lucky figured, with Richie's wife. Ronnie looked thirties, with permed hair framing a weasel's face. Richie's *wifey* looked like a model, tall and slim and fashionably overdressed for a cashier.

They looked up at Lucky's smiling approach. *Thirty seconds in.*

AT THE PALACE, there were still two old men finishing up in a back booth near the kitchen when Loo Ga entered. He noticed the waiter taking their leftovers into the kitchen for take-home cartons, so he assumed they'd paid their check.

At the cashier counter was an overweight man with his gelled hair combed back over a round Buddha face. *Richie Chow*, Loo Ga presumed. The woman next to him looked like a starlet, someone you'd see in a Hong Kong movie magazine. *Ronnie Chow's wife.*

The plan was to order takeout, a big order, paying in advance to put them at ease. Jojo and Cowboy, looking more like immigrant laborers, would enter a minute later. He had a takeout list in his head, pricey items that the kitchen could surely turn out in fifteen minutes. Three orders of everything, three being a magic number—three men, the three of them. *Imperial fried rice. Jumbo shrimp in black bean sauce. Emperor's steak kow with snow peas, baby shrimp with cashews. A hundred-and-fifty-dollar challenge he knew the kitchen would rise to, a quick slick way to end the day. But more important, it kept them all in the kitchen together.*

He plunked down two hundred-dollar bills, *lung ha touh* lobster heads, onto the counter, and smiled at the pretty cashier and Richie. She figured the change as the waiter handed off the leftovers and returned with the last takeout order of the night to the kitchen.

"*Ngoy mai,*" Lucky said, pointing to a takeout menu. As she handed him the paper menu he saw their gaze shift to what he knew was the quiet entrance of the Lam brothers. *More takeout dollars* in Ronnie's greedy eyes. Lucky pretended to peruse the menu while keeping an eye on Ronnie.

Short Lam approached the cashier counter as Tall Lam

stood between them and the entrance to the kitchen. Lucky continued to smile at Richie's *wifey* as Short Lam drew his Browning .45 and *chik-cock* chambered a round.

Ronnie's eyes went big as silver dollars as Tall Lam flapped open his raincoat to show the sawed-off Mossberg hanging off a shoulder strap underneath. Short Lam turned his gun on Ronnie who was afraid now to challenge the shotgun or the short man brandishing the big pistol.

Short Lam glanced around, saw no one exit the kitchen, and flicked the gun barrel in the cashier's direction.

"I'd hate for him to put a bullet in your pretty face, *leng nui*," Lucky said with a grin. "Call your *lo gung*."

"My *husband?*" she asked, fearful and confused.

"Do it *now*. Tell him to do as he's told and no one gets hurt."

She glanced at Ronnie's terrified face, took out her cell phone, and breathlessly made the call.

THE STARLET CASHIER gave Loo Ga his change as the last customers left the restaurant. Loo Ga kept the smile on his face even as he saw peripherally Jojo and Cowboy coming through the door. Jojo openly waved a Palace Express paper menu, the kind the restaurant included with takeout deliveries, and looked ready to order some fast food. Cowboy lingered near the door, *a lumpy laborer*. Blocking the action with his body, he flipped the door sign to CLOSED.

"One more thing," Loo Ga said. Richie also kept his smile on.

"Yes?" the lovely *lo por* asked.

"Call your *lo gung*," he said as he drew his Luger and Jojo unsheathed an oily two-foot machete. She looked ready to panic.

"Don't do anything stupid," Loo Ga warned. "Do as you're told and no one gets killed."

"Who the fuck are *you?*" Richie challenged. "We're already protected by the Ghosts."

"Well, that don't mean shit right now, does it?" Loo Ga said with a sneer.

"The *hell* it doesn't," he protested. "You'll never get away with this."

"Yeah, heard *that* before," Jojo snickered, recalling Charley Joe's words.

"Call your *lo gung*," Loo Ga repeated, his face turning stone cold. "Do it *now.*"

She looked at Richie, whose phone jingled a Hong Kong tune out of his pocket.

"Answer it, jerkoff!" Jojo ordered, slapping the long nasty blade against the side of the counter.

Richie pulled his phone out.

"Call!" Loo Ga pressed the starlet wifey again. She imagined it like a Hong Kong triad movie, *da da sot sot,* and tried to calm herself. Finally, with trembling hands, she did as she was told.

"BUT WE ALREADY paid up this month," Ronnie whined as his cell phone dittied out a jingle.

"Answer it!" Lucky ordered. He watched Ronnie

taking deep breaths as he listened to the chirping pleas from his wife.

"Yes," he answered haltingly. "Yes, they're here. Yes! Anything!" He hung up and quickly led Lucky to a hidden office behind the photo wall of Chinese land-scapes.

"Please don't let them hurt my *lo por*," Ronnie pleaded, working the safe dial with sweaty fingers.

"Hurry the fuck up, *lun yeung*!" Lucky checked his watch. *Seven minutes in. Like clockwork.* He shoved Ronnie to the carpet as the safe door swung open.

"Face down, fucker! Don't even look!" He scooped out the safe's contents. *Piece of cake.*

RICHIE'S FACE TURNED white with fear and disbe-lief as his precious wife's voice begged, "*Lo gung,* if you love me do as you're told!" Before he could ask anything, a man's voice growled from her phone.

"Give my men the money and no one gets hurt. No games, no bullshit. Fuck up and it's on *you.*"

"Yes! Okay!" he agreed as the line went dead. "Fuck! Fuckin' fuck!" as he led Loo Ga to the cash.

LUCKY BREEZED OUT of the Canton Gourmet with a big black trash bag, flashing a smile and a nod to Rich-ie's *lo por* on the way out. The Lam brothers closed out the raid behind him. It was easy for armed men to resist the urge to run and draw attention. After all, they had weapons and could discourage any pursuit.

He saw the Regal up ahead, knew its powerful engine would whisk them to the Lams' garage. Glancing behind him, he saw the Lams crossing the street, Tall Lam bringing up the rear.

His watch timer whistled. *Ten minutes.*

Then he heard screeching tires. A yellow car—a Camaro—rounded the corner and slowed near the Gourmet. Whoops from inside the muscle car.

Yellow Camaro, he mused. *Cigarette Boy drove one like that.*

"What the *fuck?*" cursed a voice Lucky recognized as belonging to *dailo* Loy Sung. Someone pointed out the car window at Tall Lam.

"The *fuck* you doing around here?"

Lucky paused at the Regal, opened the rear door. He drew the Taurus and waited for Short Lam. They watched as Tall Lam swung the Mossberg out from his raincoat and leveled a blast at the Camaro, blowing out a front tire and the driver's window. He racked a second shot and saw the volley pockmark the Camaro and shatter the window of the Gourmet.

"Let's go!" yelled Lucky. Short Lam slipped into the backseat as his lanky brother turned and dashed toward the Regal.

After the thunderous shotgun blasts, Say Low was hearing *ride like the wind* screaming in his head and knew he had to remain calm, *like the illegal street racers waiting for the green light at Cross Bay Boulevard.*

Lucky climbed into the passenger seat as curses erupted from the Camaro.

Short Lam hopped in and Tall Lam was the last one, folding into the Regal's backseat and slamming the door as the car pulled away, Say Low coolly gunning the getaway.

BACK AT THE Lams' garage, Loo Ga was surprised.

"No fuckin' shit!" he exclaimed. "Loy Sung's crew?"

"Think so," said Lucky.

"Ronnie made a call?"

"Even if he did, they couldn't have arrived so fast."

"Jerkoff Richie pitched a bitch but we made it out, no problem."

"Maybe it was just coincidence."

"Yeah, but now they'll be looking out. They see your car?"

"Not sure. Say Low moved out pretty quick."

"They didn't follow?"

"Nah, Tall Lam took care of *that*."

"Haha. That fuckin' shotgun, boy."

They poured out the bundles of cash as the others gathered around. Say Low and Jadine got five thousand each for driving. More money came out of the Canton Gourmet so the split reflected that.

The Lams pocketed ten thousand each. Cowboy and Jojo both got eight thousand.

Lucky and Loo Ga scored twenty thousand each, *dailo's pay*.

HE RETURNED TO the Asia Manor with his share of the loot. After dropping a tab of ecstasy, he stashed the cash in the duffel with the weapons. As the chemicals mixed into his blood he reflected on what he'd accomplished.

He'd slapped them all: Charley Joe and the On Yee, the Ghost Legion, and the Canton Group. He'd put the Wo faction on notice too, ripping off the Temple Garden.

Enough of sending messages, he thought, chasing the ecstasy with a swallow of XO. The only thing that could keep him from banging his way back into Chinatown was if the On Yees and the Wos paid him off—two million dollars for their *precious* notebook listing police payoffs and triad assassinations. The price would include him disappearing from New York. And not in a *bad* way.

Fuck them, he thought. The price was cheap, *peanuts* in the global sense of criminal enterprise.

Or they could counter with a million, which he'd take, and pay off his new crew before taking his talents elsewhere.

The XO swirled in his brain and he imagined money on the table again, a big room full of gamblers and criminals.

Perfect, he thought.

Video

RONNIE AND RICHIE brought the videotapes from their restaurants for a private viewing in the On Yee assembly hall, arranged by Charley Joe and Dup Choy.

In attendance were Woo Sik Kee, Kenny "Cigarette" Boy, and Ghost *dailos* Loy Sung and Taiwan. Two Wo triad officers stood in the back, looking at the two TV sets they'd placed side by side.

Charley Joe ran the tapes simultaneously, showing clearly the coordinated robberies of the two restaurants. Although cued almost a minute apart, the videos showed six armed men, in two groups of three, raiding the two restaurants near closing time.

"It's Lucky," said Charley Joe.

"And that faggot Jojo," added Dup Choy.

"The motherfuckers threatened my wife!" said Richie.

"They took more than eighty thousand from us," Ronnie said. "Money that's tied up with the credit union."

"*Dai gor* Loo Ga too," said Taiwan, "from the old days."

"The tall guy, and the short guy? They're brothers," added Loy Sung. "They're the guys we ran outta College Point."

"*That's* the guy who broke my nose!" yelled Woo Sik Kee when he recognized Cowboy.

"They're driving a black car, full size," offered Cigarette. "Older model."

"Twenty thousand on each one! *Yee mon!*" declared one of the Wo triads, upping the bounty all around.

They considered forming a posse. Dup Choy wanted to lead a handpicked On Yee crew. The Wo clan wanted to bring in people from out of town, and the Canton group pushed for the Ghost Legion, whom they were already paying for *protection*.

Arrayed against the Lucky Eight would be Dup Choy's select hitmen, the Ghost crews under *dailos* Taiwan and Loy Sung, and the Wo's long-distance guns. They were finally faced with having to deal with *dailo* Lucky, not only over the robberies but because he also still had their *notebook* listing twenty years of payoffs and assassinations.

News and Clues

HIS PHONE HUMMED, Vincent Chin's number.

"Hey, Chin," Jack greeted.

"Got another story from my Queens stringer that might interest you."

"Okay, *shoot*."

"He wrote it as an 'Emergency Response' piece."

"Right."

"Last night, around ten forty-five, calls to 911 from the Rego Park area. Reports of explosions prompted local responses by NYPD, Consolidated Edison, and EMS. No problems found at Con Ed substations, but NYPD reported that a car nearby was damaged and a Chinese restaurant had its window blown out." Vincent paused, giving Jack a chance to digest the news.

"The Chinese restaurant?"

"Called the Canton Gourmet. 1888 Austin Avenue."

"The car?"

"Unofficially, a yellow muscle car." *Gang boyz*, figured Jack. *Rolling in the 112th Precinct.*

"Anything else?"

"That's it, *chaai lo*," Vincent said, and chuckled before hanging up.

* * *

He called it his lunch hour, drove out to Rego Park. The only thing he could reasonably be sure of was the 911 calls received between 10:44 and 10:46 P.M. The stringer's blurb said *Area residents reported hearing two or three explosions and feared the nearby electrical substations had overloaded and exploded again. Con Edison techs responded but no damage was found. NYPD responded but declined comment on the continuing investigation.* PD dispatch had notified patrol and officers responded by 2249 hours, *10:49* P.M.

They watched as the workmen hefted the new glass window off the truck. Jack didn't see the words *Canton Gourmet* anywhere and figured they'd stencil that in later. *Different trades.*

"I heard an explosion," said Ronald Chow, manager of the Canton Gourmet. "And then another one, and the window blew up. We were closing at the time. It was a shock. That's all I know. I already told this to the police."

"And you don't have a security camera, something pointed toward the street?"

"No. I explained already. The recorder is being repaired."

"There was a car outside?"

"No car."

"A yellow car?"

"I don't know. Didn't see any car."

"No *bong jai* around?" The *gang-boy* reference seemed to baffle Chow, and while he searched for an answer, Jack knew he was hiding something.

"I don't know," Ronald managed to repeat.

Jack gave him his detective's card.

"Call me if you remember anything else."

He watched as the glaziers set the new picture window in place and started to seal the edges.

"It's good you have insurance," Jack said. Ronald nodded and shrugged.

"You always need to have insurance," Jack said, "but the price keeps going up, doesn't it?"

Ronald shook his permed head, kept his stone face on.

"Anyway, what can you *do?*" Jack asked. "Pray for peace, or *pay* for peace?" Jack felt Ronald Chow was being evasive, the Chinaman *who dint see nothing, dint know nothing*. And that was the way Jack left him, ignorant.

THE POLICE REPORT was just as sketchy. When patrol arrived there were no witnesses. Victims had no idea who the perpetrators were. No surveillance tape from the business owner, the Chinese restaurant.

Outside the Canton Gourmet restaurant, patrol found a disabled car, with a flat tire and broken window, and marked with heavy shot. *Not bird shot or skeet shot. Buck-shot but bigger.* Officers noticed several pellets embedded in the car's side panels. A yellow 1990 Chevy Camaro, claimed driver Kin Hung Lee, *who also claimed to have no idea who the shooter might be.*

They were permitted to drive the car to the nearest gas station to change the tire.

And the nearest one was?

THE SUNOCO ON North Street near the highway was four blocks away, and the Sikh attendant *did* have a working security videotape setup, due no doubt to having been robbed multiple times. His tape showed the yellow Camaro pulling in at 11:03 P.M. with three Chinese men getting out and changing the left front tire. One of them is seen sweeping pieces of glass from the rear section.

The license plate was clear enough.

Jack believed one of the men was at the hospital when he took custody of Lucky. *An older On Yee man, maybe a Wo, riding with Ghost gang boys? What's the connection?* The young men might deal weed, or ecstasy, or club drugs like coke, but usually the older men, *triad members*, dealt in heroin, cheaper and more plentiful now, to every junkie *chasing the dragon.*

On the drive back into Manhattan, he considered what he had tumbling in his head: a shot-out restaurant window and a shot-up muscle car. Along the way, he had a Wo old-timer, an On Yee handler, and an enforcer. He was waiting for the DMV check on Kin Hung Lee to come through but figured him for gang boy all the way.

There'd been violence but no crimes. People with dirty hands and consciences never heard or saw anything, but the violence reminded him of Lucky's style. *Unexpected. Well timed. Minimal casualties.*

Let's see how that works out! Jack mused.

* * *

THE PLATE NUMBER on the Camaro and the driver's license of Kin "Kenny" Hung Lee were up to date, no problem. The problem was Kenny had two strikes on his youthful-offender record and was on probation. Having his car shot up wouldn't look too good in his parole officer's eyes, and he'd be headed back to Riker's Island.

Jack went to the home address on Kenny's rap sheet and roused him. Feeling trapped, Kenny coughed up the answers quickly.

"We wuz just cruisin', making the rounds. We came to the restaurant and *dailo* yelled at a coupla guys on the street. He challenged them and one of them started shooting. Everyone ducked low."

"How many shots?"

"Two, I think."

"Which *dailo*?"

"Guy called Loy Sung. He got out and took aim but they took off."

"What kind of car?"

"A black car, older model, like a Riviera but cheaper. Maybe a used Regal."

"How do you *know* that? It was dark out, wasn't it?"

"I *know* my cars, man! Night *or* day, nothing outruns my Camaro."

Jack wasn't about to debate cars but was willing to bet that Billy's souped-up Mustang could give the Camaro a run for its money.

"So what happened at the restaurant?"

"Got their window shot up?"

"Don't fuck with me, boy. It won't look too cool when I perp-walk you in front of your homies."

Kenny shook his head and sighed.

"They got robbed."

"How do you know that?"

"There was a meeting this morning. At the On Yee Association. They had videotapes."

"Tapes from the restaurant?"

"Both restaurants."

"*Both?*"

"The other restaurant, in Jackson Heights."

"Who were the robbers?"

"It was *dailo* Lucky. Got a new crew."

Jack smiled, the pieces of the puzzle falling together.

"Who's in the crew?"

"He hooked up with a pimp named Jojo. And another ex–*dai gor* and three other guys. "

"What guys?"

"Don't know. They all outta Queens."

"You're not out of Queens?"

"Hell, no! I'm *all* about Manhattan, where it's hap'nin'."

"What else happened at the meeting?"

"Those boyz got a price on their heads now. And they forming a posse on them. SOS."

SOS was street slang for *Shoot on sight*.

"What else?"

"They think he's in Queens somewhere."

"What else?"

"That's all I know. They made us leave so the big shots could talk it over."

Jack gave Kenny his detective's card. "If I find out you've been lying to me, I'll be back."

Kenny nodded and frowned as Jack left him, another fish too small to keep.

When he got to the Fifth Precinct, Jack posted a Queens-wide patrol *Bolo*, a "be on lookout" cop alert for the older-model black Buick, *possibly a Regal or Riviera*. The only way to save Lucky from the gangland SOS, he knew, was if the cops got him first.

Move

THE RAIN CAME down like bullets, rattling the metal frames of the Manor's air conditioners. Outside the condo window, a somber gray overwhelmed the sky, covered the flat wet cityscape.

Lucky repacked the duffel, everything from ammo to Uzi to Mossberg snug in place. He carried the Beretta in a holster clipped inside his waistband. *Not your usual belly gun.* He had everything else in the Samsonite rollaway, his fast-lane life reduced to compact luggage and a ready-to-go duffel.

He'd found a rental apartment in Gramercy Park and paid a month's cash advance. Having found a place near Chinatown, his focus narrowing, he planned to change the door lock and stash everything there.

He'd leave the Regal on the back lot of the Asia Manor. They'd need a *van jai* for the next job, a hit, grab and run across the rooftops. Unlike the gambling basements on Mott Street, where they could escape through the *unlocked* connecting back alleys, courtesy of Cowboy's construction master keys, the Tsun Jin gambling hall was on the second floor of a four-story building on the Lower East Side. The escape plan would be a rooftop dash toward Allen Street, and down some back stairs to street level. Say Low would be waiting in a step van.

THE RENTAL APARTMENT was located just above the hubbub of the East Village and farther north of the housing projects of Alphabet City. Nestled on Seventeenth Street, the apartment was far enough west from Irving Place to go unnoticed. *A floor-through space in an old brownstone building, and more important, within striking distance of Chinatown.*

He hadn't forgotten the bottle of XO, took a slug of it in the kitchenette cove and considered the layout of the Tsun Jin association's gambling club.

Until Tall Lam let loose with the shotgun, they hadn't had to fire a shot, which meant the chance of his luck running out got bigger with each endeavor. But he needed to show his kickass bravado, bring the Ghost Legion back in line, or die trying.

He didn't expect to take down a thriving gambling house with less than his crew of eight, including Say Low driving the getaway van and Jadine in a backup car. But the logistics intrigued him. It could be another easy score, another notch for the crew, if everything went right.

Cowboy would disable the rudimentary rooftop door locks of the adjacent buildings along the escape dash. In Chinatown, those locks would have been the simple hook-and-latch variety. If necessary, he could use his contractor's credentials.

Short Lam ordered earplugs for everyone, almost

military grade and used by hunters and target shooters. Enough noise reduction—*108 decibels*—for shotguns but good enough for the flash-bang grenades too. *Made in the USA*. He'd painted the plug ends with a flesh-colored nail polish, making them almost undetectable in-ear.

Jadine, playing Short Lam's girlfriend, would smuggle in the flash-bangs, and Cowboy's little gun, between her legs under her knee-length skirt. She'd leave them under the trash bucket in the toilet room. Short Lam would have his army .45 duct-taped to his inner thigh, and a paratrooper knife nestled in the small of his back under his loose rain parka. A half hour later, Jadine would bounce as Cowboy arrived.

Two inside men in place, acting like they don't know each other. Taking up positions after trips to the men's toilet. Cowboy, scoping the back door. Short Lam watching the dealers, the control room. Loo Ga would enter with his Luger and target the managers.

Lucky would follow shortly, with Jojo and Tall Lam in tow. The two most wanted backed by Mr. Silent.

He figured the raid a *150*, a hundred-fifty-grand hit on a holiday gambling weekend in Chinese New York City.

It was the last stepping stone to Mott Street.

Hello Goodbye

HE DIDN'T MIND walking the two blocks from Eighth Avenue where the *sai ba* minibus had deposited him. The walking distance gave him space to breathe, clear his head. Just across the East River, his Sunset Park condo was still far enough from Chinatown and the Lower East Side to give him a sense of escape and a hint of hope.

By the time he reached his building, he sensed another presence, like a long tail following him. *No one else on the street, though.* Before he could key the lobby door, he heard Lucky's disembodied voice.

"Not bad, kid." He'd forgotten he'd given Lucky his address. "Good to get out of Chinatown, huh? Too bad you had to *cop out* to get here."

Tat's face appeared suddenly and ghostly from the shadows, framed by the cropped haircut that Chinatown gang boys favored, long on top, tight on the sides. The thickset body that followed next was vintage Lucky, a brawler's body; he'd gained back the twenty pounds he'd lost in the coma.

"Nice building tho. *Shiny.* No roaches. No stink. Got a good lease, I hope." Lucky nodded toward the side street where Jack followed. In the dark alley, Lucky fired up a cigarette. "Heard you busted my car," he said.

"Heard *you've* been busting heads," answered Jack. Lucky laughed, a long-ago teenage laugh.

"Heard you were looking for me."

"Ha, I'm not the only one."

"Well, here I am. What the fuck you need, *boy?*" he said with a smile.

"You still got a chance to get out."

"Not the *witless protection* again, *puhleeze.*"

"I can get you out alive."

"And I can get you a promotion, right?"

"You got problems with the On Yee? The Wos? I can help."

"Don't need help."

"I can have their cars towed."

"Like you did *mine?*"

"I can have their businesses cited. Issue summonses. Get them violated."

"Don't need none of that."

"Need you to change your attitude. Save your own life."

"We *had* this talk already. But here's some cheap advice. Stay the fuck out of Chinatown business. You ain't built for it and you'll just get hurt. Fuckin' cops only get in the way."

"Guess I'll see you in a box at Wah Fook then."

"Guess I'll see you on Mott Street when you come down for your weekly red envelope." He dropped the cigarette, crushed it under his heel. "*Come* my way, *every* day will be Chinese New Year's, bro. The streets are paved with gold, remember?" He turned and quickly stepped toward a dark car idling lights off halfway down the street.

Jack wondered if the driver was Jojo or another of Lucky's new crew. The sedan was off and away before he could get a good look at the rear plates. *You'll only get in the way,* he heard his boyhood friend warning. *Stay the fuck out.*

HAKKA Pre-synced

THE TSUN JIN association was an old-school tong, a Chinatown civic association that was also a front for racketeers within their own vast Hakkanese membership.

They'd organized in the 1920s and had since maintained chapters globally: Hong Kong, Taiwan, Macao. Britain, France, Brazil. From Holland to Canada. In America, Tsung Jin operated chapters in Honolulu, San Francisco, New York City, Philadelphia, and Washington.

Besides the gambling basement in their headquarters building on Division Street, they'd also expanded into high-stakes gambling games at a gambling hall on the edge of Chinatown. Word was that the Tung Sin faction was leading them toward the *baak fun*, chasing the dragon.

For an organization that began with noble patriotic and military fervor, their main focus now was their myriad criminal moneymaking enterprises: gambling, loan sharking, extortion, dealing in illegal cigarettes and alcohol, immigrant trafficking, drugs, and contract murder.

Unlike the Fifth Precinct, which was mostly

Chinatown and Chinese, the Seventh included housing projects—the Rutgers, Baruch, Vladeck, and LaGuardia Houses—and the low-rent Lower East Side, twenty thousand poor and working-class people, mostly black and Puerto Rican.

Friday and Saturday nights were the busiest for the Seventh Precinct patrol cops, with the minority inner-city enclaves blowing off a week's worth of steam. Sometimes the steam turned to hot blood.

THEY FELL IN behind a small group of gamblers waiting to be buzzed in.

When they got to the second-floor door they would appear to be an odd couple: the older short guy with the young ditzy girlfriend, *like an uncle dating his niece*. Short Lam and Jadine passed the door goons with barely a second look. *Aiyah weird people love to gamble*.

The room was smoky and the stark fluorescent strip lights overhead gave it a prison feel. There was loud banter from the rear table.

Short Lam took it all in like it was slow motion—the ceremonial plaques high up on the walls, black-and-white photos of the Old Village, the Venerable Elders—his view drifting along to the big mirrored window of the control room at the far end.

He estimated the crowd at the tables to be around forty people, early yet for the night crawlers but just before the end of every midnight waiter's shift. With Jadine on his arm, he made a bet at the first table.

Win or lose, they'd make three bets, play three hands, before moving on to the second table. He knew they were being videotaped from somewhere. They'd accept the complimentary shots of Johnny Red. Jadine would *accidentally* spill her drink on herself and then go to the toilet where she would place the flash-bangs and Cowboy's gun under the trash bin.

He won the first bet and Jadine clapped her hands like a silly schoolgirl. The hard-core around her were not amused.

COWBOY LOOKED THICK and goofy and went along good-naturedly as they patted him across the shoulders and back before letting him through. *He knew he was clean*, so easy to play along. *Easy enough access. What else could they do anyway, fondle my balls?*

He saw Short Lam and Jadine in place at the second table, playing high-low, and colors.

He placed a bet for appearances. Win or lose he was going to the piss room to retrieve his gun.

Loo Ga arrived a minute later, a Chinese logo on his company windbreaker and work pants. He looked and acted like a Chinese plumber who'd just gotten paid and was ready to throw down a paycheck's worth of bets.

They never suspected he'd have a Luger strapped under his balls.

His arrival was Jadine's cue to leave, go back to the car and wait. She *mistakenly* exited through the front door, distracting the guards just enough so Loo Ga faded easily into the crowd, a fistful of dollars in his gun hand.

Game set, he thought, making his first bet.

Three armed men on the inside.

Three more come to the door.

The flash-bang stuns the crowd.

The shotgun and Uzi break out.

IT HAD STARTED to rain, a light drizzle.

They looked like two waiters and a kitchen helper fresh off the midnight shift. Lucky wore a deliveryman's parka, and Jojo left his little black waiter's bow tie dangling off his collar. Tall Lam ambled along in his dirty *da-jop* kitchen smock, with the sawed-off shotgun on a shoulder sling snug against his ribs.

At the second-floor entrance, Lucky liked what he saw: Loo Ga ahead to the right, and Cowboy at the far end on the left near the exit.

Jojo and Tall Lam ready behind him.

He smirked and took a boxer's breath through his nose.

The two door goons were cockeyeing him before abruptly turning to the sound of Short Lam's shout from the toilet door. Something flew through the air and landed on the middle table as the toilet door slammed shut.

There was a confused hush from the gamblers.

Lucky turned away just as the room exploded into blinding light and concussive force. *Playing cards and poker chips twisting in the air. The smell of magnesium mixing with the cigarette and cigar smoke.*

Fuck yeah for the earplugs. He slugged one of the wobbly guards, knocking him out. He pocketed a revolver off him as Tall Lam took three steps in and swung the shotgun out from his smock. He aimed at the ceiling and squeezed the trigger.

The blast blew out chunks of the ceiling panels, and anyone who hadn't gotten the hint from the flash-bang grenade dove to the floor in terror.

Jojo took a knife off the second guard and kicked him under one of the tables.

Tall Lam racked the shotgun again.

Several men lay moaning under the tables but everyone else scuttled and crawled toward the wall, where they huddled together.

Short Lam came out of the toilet and helped Cowboy drop the exit guards as Loo Ga scooped money off the tables.

Tall Lam calmly let another blast rip, shattering the control room's two-way mirror window. Someone there yelled something in Hakkanese and a wild shot rang out from the room.

Lucky ripped off a burst of Uzi fire that raked a jagged pattern of bullet holes across the front of the control window. *No one fucks with an Uzi.*

"Go!" he yelled, joining Loo Ga and Short Lam as they rushed the control room. Jojo and Cowboy covered everyone else as Tall Lam smiled, racked again for the third shot.

Inside the control room, two men lay on the floor, one

apparently unconscious, the other bleeding from a shoulder wound. A third man cowered in the corner.

Lucky yanked the terrified man off the floor, shoved him against the wall. The man cried out as Lucky smacked him across the head with the barrel of the Beretta. He was whimpering as Lucky pressed the pistol against his ear.

"Money or die!" he growled, cocking back the nine-millimeter's hammer.

The dealer-manager—*whatever the fuck*—saw death in Loo Ga's eyes and spun the safe's dial with shaky fingers. He yanked the door open and fell back as Jojo shoved fat stacks of money into a duffel bag.

Feeling like $100K, Lucky snatched up the duffel, zipped it. He stepped out of the room as the rest of the crew closed ranks around him. They were under fifteen minutes. Backing their way out, Loo Ga at the rear exit now. *Stairway to the roof. The fire escape if needed.* Duffel in one hand, Uzi in the other. Jojo behind him, with Cowboy watching the sides as the Lam brothers covered their escape.

The table nearest the entrance suddenly overturned, errant gunshots erupting from behind it. In their crouching retreat, the middle table also flipped onto its side, some other Hakka playas coming alive now.

Tall Lam shredded the first tabletop with a direct blast, blowing through it like it was cardboard. Lucky splintered the second table bursting off the rest of the clip in the Uzi. *Cries from behind the tables.* Short Lam's Browning barking out forty-fives added to Jojo's nine-millimeter firepower as they spread out around the exit.

There was no return fire this time. Taking advantage of the lull, several gamblers scrambled out the front door. There was yelling and then a gunshot from the stairs.

Lucky slung the money duffel over his shoulder and put his last clip into the Uzi. He took a last look at the terrified gamblers huddled against the opposite wall, and kicked open the back door.

Swinging out into the hallway, the metal door took several heavy bullets as Lucky gave Short Lam the nod. Lam pulled the pin on the flash-bang grenade, crouched behind the door and tossed it toward the front stairwell.

There was a blast from behind him. *Tall Lam giving table two some extra cover fire.* Then the hallway erupted as the flash-bang exploded.

"Go!" Lucky yelled, angling the Uzi behind the door edge and burping off the full clip as Loo Ga darted out. There was no return fire and Lucky bolted after him, the Beretta in his gun hand on the way up.

He heard Jojo yelling something from below.

They were almost to the fourth floor when the door to the corner apartment at the top of the stairs cracked open. Loo Ga took aim, hesitated. They ducked as gunfire flared out of the dark apartment.

There was a shotgun blast from downstairs.

"Down!" Lucky yelled, jamming off six nine-millimeter hollow points that forced the shooter's door to close.

Go! signaled Lucky, and Loo Ga ran up the last flight of

stairs to the roof. Lucky kept his gun on the door as he followed past, backing his way up the stairs. *Gunfire from floors below.* He couldn't tell if it was from the gambling hall or the stairwell. *Another blast from down there. A real gunfight.*

Where was Jojo? he wondered. *And Short Lam?*

Yelling from the stairwell. He could almost feel the footsteps thundering up.

"Come on!" Loo Ga gestured frantically. Lucky tossed him the money duffel and slipped a fresh clip into the Beretta before following him onto the roof. They moved away from the door toward the adjacent rooftop, Loo Ga leading now with Lucky looking back for Jojo and the others.

He took a breath, waited a moment. Loo Ga waving at him—*Come on!*—from the third rooftop. Halfway to Grand Street.

Cowboy? The Lam brothers should be pulling out by now.

He imagined the wail of police sirens in the dark night distance and started after Loo Ga. After a few steps he glanced back and saw the roof door open again. *About time*, he thought, expecting Jojo or Cowboy.

But the figure that stepped out crouched into a combat stance and started firing at them. A second figure emerged and joined him.

Where the fuck was Jojo?

He waved Loo Ga forward and faded back, drawing the attackers to the Eldridge Street side of the rooftops. He knew he had a full clip in the Beretta, and though the Uzi was useless now, he also had the door guard's revolver.

Best to get to a neutral spot between them and the Grand Street rooftop.

The two attackers split up, ducking behind the low walls that separated the buildings. *Don't get caught in a cross fire, and keep them in front.* He drifted back along the roof ledge knowing he could hold them off until the others appeared.

Loo Ga called out, already at Grand Street three buildings away.

Ahead of Lucky were the pitch-black Chinatown rooftops, slick with rain from the moonless sky, the only lights twinkling in the far distance from the high windows of Confucius Towers, and the dim foggy glow of the scattered streetlamps forty feet below.

The inky distance included chimneys and exhaust ducts, blocky skylights and hallway sheds that made everything a menacing silhouette, providing plenty of cover over the remaining forty yards of blacktop.

He drew the captured revolver from his pocket and carried it lefty, starting a two-gun retreat as gunshots exploded from his left, behind some exhaust ducts. Expecting shots from his right, he held his fire and ducked behind a chimney stack.

Another single shot from his left. *A revolver? Like the shooter was saving his shots?*

Pau papau! rapid fire from his right. He could feel the bullets whizzing by him. A dark shape advanced boldly over a low wall, caught in the flash of his own gun barrel. *A semiauto pistol . . .*

Lucky leaned out from the other edge of the chimney

and emptied the Beretta. The dark shape fell with a thud, the man squeezing off three shots into the air before the pistol fire stopped for good.

The Beretta was empty now and he tossed it, shifting the Hakka's revolver to his right hand. He backed away from the chimney keeping his view open and his focus to his left. *The second shooter. Where?*

A shot roared from his right, less than ten feet away. He rapid-fired until he heard the dry click of the empty revolver. Turning, he tossed the gun off the roof and sprinted along the edge. He hurdled the low wall toward the roof door on Grand Street, breathless as another volley rang out behind him.

Say Low, he pictured, *waiting in the van*.

The roof door just a short zigzag away.

The others went to Jadine's backup in the Suburban?

Loo Ga waiting for him?

ComeBack

IT .ALWAYS STARTED slowly, with the deep drumbeat of dread in his head, followed by the clash of metal, cymbals and gongs, and the insistent cry of the cell phone or pager. Calling from the dead of night, the killing hours between midnight and 5 A.M., a night-crawler tour fueled by alcohol and despair, anger and violence.

An urgent dispatcher's voice. *Manhattan South.*

"We got a hot shoot, respond to 49 Hester Street. Fifth Precinct."

A Hester Street address, *back to Chinatown*, the place that no longer claimed his body but was still recalling his soul. He shook the sleepy fatigue from his head, rolled his neck and popped the ligaments. He pulled on his clothes, grabbing the parka that held a disposable plastic camera and his service weapon.

Adrenaline pumping, he jogged down to Eighth Avenue and jumped into one of the Chinese *see gay* cars that lined up near the all-night noodle shacks. He badged the driver, giving him the address in Cantonese while slipping him a ten-spot.

"Go!" ordered Jack. "*Faai di* hurry!"

The driver slipped through the shortcuts and weaved

the black car across the Brooklyn Bridge, arriving at the corner of Hester and Allen in seventeen screeching minutes. Jack slipped the driver another Hamilton.

From the service car he could see the flashing lights of the emergency vans leaving the scene, whooping their way back with the weekend wounded. *He'd have to follow up later.*

An old fat sergeant ambled over as Jack approached the building, sizing him up.

"You *Yu?*" he asked with a smirk.

"Break it down, Sarge," Jack said humorlessly flashing his badge. "Whaddya got?"

The grin came off the fat cop's face.

"I was working traffic on Delancey so I was nearby when the call went out. When I got here there were *Chinamen* running out of the building everywhere, and two of them laying on the sidewalk."

Jack ignored the *Chinaman* bait, had no time for barbs with a cop reduced to directing traffic at midnight.

"I called for backup. Two EMTs arrived first and tended to the wounded. Some others ran out the back, I think. It was too dark to see."

"What time was this?"

"Twenty-four-thirty, something. About twelve-thirty."

"Go on."

"Backup arrived. Fifth squad. A car from the Seventh."

"That's it?"

"Well, Lower SpicTown jumped off tonight—Kings and Crips—guess that's all they could spare."

"Then what?"

"Then we went up, knocking on doors, the whole nine. Nobody spoke much English and no one saw anything." Jack shook his head, knowing the immigrant reluctance to get involved with the police. Especially *gwai lo* white police.

"Now we got it covered front and back. Two guys checking the back alleys on the street."

"How many wounded?"

"Two, far as I could tell. A few declined medical attention."

"Where're they now?"

"Dunno. They left when we went upstairs." He caught Jack's frown.

"How many dead?"

"Four. All *Chi*-nese. ME's been notified. Just waiting on the wagons now."

"Let's go," Jack said, his adrenaline juicing him as the sergeant followed him into the building.

He caught his breath at the top of the long flight of stairs, stood in the open door and took out the throwaway camera. He'd always wanted his own impressions of a crime scene, didn't like depending solely on the CSI technicians.

There were bullet holes everywhere, shattered glass, obliterated wood tables. Gambling debris, cards, and plastic chips scattered about. The air smelled of burned metal and tobacco and blood.

He framed the shots in his mind.

Behind one of the perforated wood tables, a male body lay lifeless, bleeding out from multiple frontal wounds. There was an empty thirty-eight-caliber revolver by his side. *A wide shot.* He brought the camera closer. *Chinese. Fortyish.* The snapshot better than a chalk outline.

The second body was in a narrow room at the far end, behind the shattered mirrored-glass window—an old man slumped beneath a table. Jack didn't see any physical trauma, and there was no blood on him at all. The medics had *pronounced* him. Later, the examiner would figure out the *how* and *why*.

On the table was a cracked video recorder that looked like it'd caught a couple of pellets from a shotgun. He took pictures anyway, figuring to *check it on the way back.*

In the hallway outside the back door, the sergeant pointed upstairs.

"One on the steps," he sounded winded. "And one on the roof. Can't miss 'em." He started back down the stairs.

"Gotta check on the meat wagons," he continued. "See if anything else turned up."

"Good," Jack answered carelessly. He continued up the stairs alone, which is what he preferred anyway.

THE THIRD BODY was sprawled across the steps in the stairway between the third and fourth floors. He'd been shot front and back, caught in a cross fire. *Sucka fire.* Jack stepped around him. *More snapshots.* His handsome face looked familiar, Jack recalling JoJo's driver's-license photo from the Queens precinct. *Find JoJo and you'll find Lucky*, he remembered thinking. *SOS. Shoot on sight.*

There was one more body on the roof.

On the top landing, he took a deep monk's breath, and then shouldered his way through the roof door.

At 1:30 A.M. the Chinatown rooftops were *mock* ink-black, the slang way they described it when they were teenagers. He flicked on his pocket Maglite and started across the tar. He kept to the middle, swinging his light left and right.

He'd crossed three buildings when he saw it, a bulky shape, twisted back and half-seated, a dead Chinese with an empty pistol in his hand. It wasn't Lucky.

More snapshots front and back.

In the open darkness there were no bullet holes that he could see. Some bullets might be embedded in the nearby structures but he'd have to wait for daylight to get a good look. *Another follow-up.*

He decided to go back downstairs to check the video recorder and construct his report on the carnage. He imagined the *Daily News* and the *Post* having a field day with sensational bloody headlines but hoped that Chinatown's *United National* would provide an honest Chinese point of view.

The videotape recorder was cracked in two places but was still working. The tape itself hadn't fared as well. He rewound it as far as it would go—not far, only back to 11:50 P.M.—a wide view on Chinese men gathered around tables. A grainy black-and-white picture. The scene was punctuated by a blinding flash, followed by fractured and pixelated images of a tall man firing a short shotgun, and then another man, with cropped hair and thickset body, jamming off a burst of automatic gunfire. He resembled Lucky, the bravado in his movements.

The audio had been disabled, so the violent chaos, the panicked people dashing about, the sporadic gunfire and the overturned tables, was silently understated. He imagined the large bursts of gunfire sounding like fireworks on Chinese New Year.

The tape captured the raiders retreating through the back door, with Lucky carrying a duffel bag, then pandemonium before the screen went to snow and static.

He swept the scene again.

For his cop transgressions, he'd been sent to mop up a Chinatown bloodbath, assigned to tally up and explain the body count. *A Chinese detective managing a major crime investigation.* He knew they were putting a yellow face on it.

Forensics would map and detail the hundreds of rounds fired, the different-caliber bullets involved, the types of firearms recovered.

The medical examiner would autopsy the dead and explain how they died.

But what was clear from what he saw, and knew, was that the cause of all the deaths and injuries was a robbery gone bad. A robbery of an illegal gambling hall by a Chinatown gang led by an ex–Ghost Legion *dailo* nicknamed Lucky Louie. That Lucky was a boyhood friend, a Chinatown blood brother, wasn't supposed to matter.

He knew the surviving members of Lucky's crew were in the wind, and he was sure the Hakkanese Tsun Jin, along with the On Yee posse, the Wo triads, and the Canton Group with the Ghosts, would all be in the hunt for them.

When more bodies turned up, the Chinese will have settled it *their* way once again.

"Crime Scene's here!" the sergeant yelled up from the street door.

He was ready to turn the scene over to them, set it up and break it down. It was 2 A.M. and he knew they'd take a couple of hours.

He pocketed the throwaway camera and wondered how much longer the morgue wagons would take. They'd have the body bags for the dead faces etched in his mind.

As the technicians trooped up the stairs, he was already planning another report that he knew Captain Marino wasn't going to be happy with.

Bad to Worse

HE WASN'T EXPECTING the coroner's report until midafternoon at least, but by the time he finished detailing the robbery shootout, it was daylight.

Still too early for the good captain. He left the report on the CO's desk.

He caught a short ride with a sector car to Downtown Emergency.

The wounded Hakkas had been treated and released hours ago. *What took you so long?* Neither had any health insurance and he was skeptical of the names they left. *Som Yung Kai. Dong So Wai.* Addresses he knew were Chinatown supermarkets.

He hadn't expected anything useful from them anyway.

EDDIE'S COFFEE WAS open for the 7 A.M. early birds.

He nursed a *nai cha* and a steamed *bao* at the short counter, waiting for Fook's 30-Minute Photo to open. He'd drop off the throwaway camera, and for the promise of a *bao*, Fook Junior would process his pictures first, *da jeem*, letting him cut the queue of orders.

When he got back to the Fifth station house, Captain Marino was in his office seated behind his desk. Jack's report was flapped open and dog-eared, and the Italian face the captain gave him was one you'd give to a rude child.

"I told you," he reminded, pointing his finger. "Keep him outta my precinct. Remember?"

"The Seventh Precinct was there *first*, I heard."

"Don't be a fuckin' wise guy. Already IA wants your ass on a *deluxe* just for knowing this guy in the first place. *And* you let him go? Turned him over to *you don't know who*?"

"It didn't happen that way."

"'Course not. Never does. But now people are dead because of that."

"Not true."

"Maybe could have prevented it."

"With what? After-school basketball programs?"

"The case is being turned over to OCCB anyway. *And* Immigration. *So*, you're gonna be humping a desk."

Jack took a *shaolin* breath through his nose. *Giving the case to Organized Crime Control, and ICE? Reassigning me to a desk?*

"And shutting the fuck up."

Jack's eyes went long distance and he heard Pa's bitter words. *Cop? Chaai lo ah? They use you against your own people. Like a running dog. A jouh gow.*

And Lucky's contempt—*that badge don't make you no better. Chinaman cop, first sign of trouble you're the one they throw under the bus.*

He wanted to say, *That's fuckin' bullshit,* captain, *with all due respect,* when the captain's desk phone rang. Marino listened briefly, handed the phone angrily to Jack.

"Dispatch. They found another body." He clenched his fists. "*JesusMotherMary* from bad to worse."

Jack listened intently. *Dah soopa* at 107 Eldridge. Dah Soopa? *You know, the janitor.* Oh, copy that. The super.

Eldridge Street near the crime scene.

Captain Marino gave him a *get the fuck outta my office look* so he obliged.

He left the station house without looking back.

Garbage Removal

NUMBER 107 WAS the last tenement building on the block, at the corner of Eldridge and Grand Streets. A small walkup, it nevertheless offered a convenience store on the street level. The building shared a backyard and a side alley with 222 Allen Street, a much bigger building at the other end of Grand. Parts of the common areas were fenced off and locked *to keep out the feral cats and the occasional stray dog, Chinese or otherwise.*

Number 107 was around the corner and down the block from the Tsun Jin building.

The super wasn't a big man but looked wiry and fit. *Fiftyish* from his thin gray hair. He lived in the building and acted as janitor and maintenance man, occasional painter and plumber. *A Chinese jack of all trades.*

He led Jack through a narrow hallway lined with grimy garbage cans. The smell of years of Chinatown waste had leached into the floor and walls and got more pungent as they came to the back door. He could hear Cantonese opera music from one of the apartments upstairs.

Fusing his broken English with his guttural Toishanese, the super complained.

"This one small building. Only eight *apockment*. Still too muchee garbage." He unlatched the back door.

"Keepee too muchee garbage *here*."

The super usually swapped out the full garbage bags at 9 A.M., Jack understood, *but later on weekends*. The weekend accumulation was bigger and always overflowed into the side alley waiting on the evening pickup.

"Too muchee," he repeated. "No good."

They came to a big pile of black garbage bags.

"So, I moving the bags, see the leg. The foot, *the shoe*, sticking up." He stepped to one side of the pile and pointed.

Jack followed, taking a monk's breath. It was a hiking boot, black, and lightweight with a rugged tread. Reminded him of military footwear. *It wasn't the shoes that got him killed.*

The super lifted away two bags that had fallen inward and covered the rest of the body.

Jack's heart sank immediately, his lips suddenly dry. The dead man was Lucky. *Or unlucky.*

He swallowed the sad metallic taste of his back teeth. Dead bodies didn't shake him anymore, but seeing the crumpled and broken body of his Chinatown brother hammered his toughness.

Lucky's face had a purplish tint. His eyes were open and the discoloration underscored the look of surprise. *What the fuck?* he seemed to be asking.

He had a chest wound.

Jack felt for a pulse as the super watched, and of course there wasn't one, the wrist stiff.

He glanced skyward. It looked like Lucky had fallen backward off the roof, landing on his head and shoulders five stories down, to the concrete of the side alley, behind a mound of garbage that scarcely broke his fall. The topmost bags had fallen back over him. Maybe that was why the uniforms had missed him on the perimeter canvas. *In the dark, even if they'd gotten past the locked gates, they wouldn't have seen him.* The exposed leg was propped on garbage and his body was doubled over and disjointed at the shoulder.

Jack's nightmares come true. In the back of his cop's mind he wanted to take pictures, but remembered he'd deposited the throwaway camera at Fook's Photo.

There was a webbed shoulder strap that wrapped behind Lucky, attached to an empty Uzi machine pistol. *Gangsta to the end.* In the raw stench, Jack took shallow breaths, shook his head, and held back the tears. *What a waste of life.* He'd always hated that helpless, hopeless feeling of being too late. The Chinatown blood brother, the cop, always *after* the fact.

The Cantonese opera, a lament, drifted out of a high window.

He checked around Lucky's body but didn't see any other items that might also have fallen from the rooftop.

"Too bad," the super said.

"Yeah, too bad," Jack said. "I can take it from here."

The Super took a last glance at Lucky, at the Uzi. "He a bad guy?"

Jack couldn't answer that, instead put on a frown and shook his head.

The super retreated back into the building, happy to have the cop clean up the mess.

Jack called the medical examiner's office. *They'd send a wagon and conduct an autopsy.* He couldn't help straddling the line between cop and friend. *A burial somewhere? Or a memorial?* Thoughts that would never have crossed his mind. *No one will claim the body, and the city would front for the cremation.*

Maybe Lucky had been right—being a cop hadn't changed anything. Chinatown criminals still settled matters their own way. *Cops just got in the way.*

He remembered Lucky's words on that dark night in Sunset Park. *Stay the fuck outta Chinatown business. You'll just get hurt.*

He went up to the roof.

The daytime view from above exposed the labyrinth of connecting backyards and side alleys that ran between buildings, fenced off or barricaded from the street.

"Keeps out the bums."

"The homeless?"

"No, the bums."

From the position of Lucky's body below, Jack figured the likely area where Lucky fell backward, trying to imagine *what happened in the dark?*

How had Lucky been shot? Staggering back before falling over the ledge?

Did Lucky kill the Hakka man on the adjacent roof?

What happened to the duffel bag he's seen carrying out of the Tsun Jin hall on the videotape?

He continued the police report in his head, Lucky's death an asterisk to the Tsun Jin robbery. He left the roof, bound for the medical examiner's office. He'd decline to *sit a desk* at the Fifth and would request two weeks' vacation time instead. The captain would approve it, everyone glad to see him out of there. *Himself included*.

He'd wrap the case and leave the paperwork on Marino's desk.

Rooney's Pub was just two blocks from the morgue, and would give him space to finish the report.

THE INITIAL CORONER'S report categorized the deaths of the two Hakkanese men, and Jojo, as gunshot homicides. The death of the old man in the little room, however, was ruled a *natural* heart-attack death. They didn't rule it *accidental*, caused by external factors. *The heart attack could have happened anywhere, anytime*. Insurance payouts were often affected by these rulings, Jack knew.

He added it to the sobering paperwork.

The report on Lucky came later, with the alcohol still medicating his pain. Lucky had suffered two gunshot wounds; a .380-caliber *through and through* in his left calf, *non-life-threatening*, and a nine-millimeter chest wound, in the heart area. They'd found traces of gunshot residue on his shirt and slicker, meaning he'd been shot at close range.

The ME ruled it a homicide but hadn't made an entry as to COD, the *cause of death*. Was it the five-story plunge that killed him? Or the nine-millimeter bullet still lodged near his heart?

Jack read a ballistics notation from one of the crime-scene technicians: 9-mm bullet is of *East German* origin, a hotter and heavier load best used in German Lugers.

A German Luger? Who the hell carries a German Luger these days? In Chinatown? The answers eluded him. He couldn't picture how Lucky could've been shot twice, then fell, or was pushed, off the roof.

As usual in Chinatown, he had a lot more questions than answers.

He knew they'd keep Lucky on ice for three days. If no one claimed the body, they'd incinerate him. *Cremation* was a nicer word for it. Pack the ashes in a carton smaller than a shoebox. *Ashes to ashes.* Another thousand dollars secured a one-foot square hole in the potter's field at Queens Calvary. They'd throw in the little footstone for free. *Dust to dust.*

He paid for the *arrangements* at the Wah Fook funeral parlor. He declined the optional Chinese-language news-paper obituary; with all the enemies Lucky had acquired, it was best not to publicize where he'd be buried. Lucky had no family *so who else is gonna burn incense for a China-town gangsta anyway?*

Even with the five-hundred-dollar *cop* discount they gave Jack, the deal still cost a few thousand he really couldn't afford but felt obligated about, *the least he could do.*

He left the Wah Fook, lighter in his wallet and heavier

in his heart. By the time he got back to Sunset Park it was late and he was exhausted. He quenched his thirst with a cold can of beer as his bed beckoned him. He was unofficially on vacation *as far as he was concerned*, and the Tsun Jin reports were already a wrap on the CO's desk.

Seventy-two hours before cremation?

His thoughts swirled and pounded but didn't keep him from oblivion when his head hit the pillow.

The only escape he had left.

Oblivion

HE WASN'T SURE if it was part of a dream or outside the oblivion—a 4 A.M. call from the *mommy* of the cathouse on Broome Street. *Lucky's first stop.*

"Meet me at Bamboo Garden, eleven o'clock." "*Yum cha*" was how she put it. He couldn't remember how he'd come to know her as Angelina or Angel Chao. *Something Billy Bow might have said?*

He crashed again, only short hours but out deep.

When he awoke, feeling well rested, he checked his phone. *Angelina's call at 4:44 A.M.* The worst numbers a superstitious Chinaman gambler could get. *It wasn't a dream after all.*

Chinatown *calling.*

THE BAMBOO GARDEN was a known Hip Ching dim sum palace, which made him wonder if *sister* Chao was protected by the Dragons, whom the Chings sponsored, and by Lucky's Ghosts as well. *Rival gangs protecting the same joint?* It was unheard of.

At 11 A.M. the place wasn't crowded yet and he took a table in the back that gave a good view of the big dining room.

The waiter brought a pot of tea.

He watched her enter, looking a lot different than how he remembered her, in a bathrobe with a towel on her head. Her hair fell shoulder length and she wore a simple black suit—no jewelry—giving a businesslike appearance.

The guy who escorted her looked more like bodyguard than pimp, and she clearly had *juice* here judging by the way the waitstaff practically kowtowed to her.

He decided to be polite, treat her with courtesy, and give her *face*.

She came to his table like a *dai gar jeer* "Big Sister" and seated herself. The muscle guy took a seat out of the way.

Jack politely poured her some hot tea as the steam-cart ladies deposited plates of dim sum. As soon as the carts rolled away and the obsequious manager's attention had died down, Angelina casually took an envelope from her LV shoulder bag and handed it to him.

She didn't seem concerned about the transaction possibly being recorded on restaurant videotape. He accepted what looked like a manila jiffy bag, sealed, the size people sent paperback books in.

"From your *si hing*, Tat."

She took a sip of tea to wet her lips but never touched the dim sum dishes. And neither did he. He pocketed the envelope, asked:

"You know what's in there?"

"No." Almost too quick an answer.

"When did he give you this?"

"A few days after. After you *visited* me."

Before the rampage, Jack mused. *Was Lucky Boy giving me a freebie from the grave? Like insurance or payback?*

"Why *now?*"

"He said to wait. After his . . . *passing*." She said it like it was a good thing.

"That's what he wanted?"

"Yes."

There was a pause, when he wondered about her connection to Lucky.

"Anything *else* I should know?" he asked pointedly.

"He said he considered you like a brother. *Si hing*."

"That's it?" He frowned.

"He said to 'remember the rooftops'. Whatever that means."

Angelina took another sip of tea and stood abruptly. Jack was caught off guard but managed to say "Thank you." He stood as her bodyguard escorted her out, as if she needed any protection in this place.

He pocketed the envelope. Leaving the untouched steamers of dim sum on the table, he headed for Confucius Towers.

The lower level of Confucius Parking was the only place nearby—quiet and isolated—that he could think of. The Paki attendants scarcely noticed as he went down.

He sat in the Mustang, the thought buzzing in his head that Angelina could have seen the contents, repackaged it and then given the envelope to him. *Whores knew all the tricks*.

He tore open the envelope, pulled out a small black

notebook, like a DayMinder, that could fit in your back pocket. The kind sold in any Chinatown stationery store. Protruding behind the cover was a folded piece of copy paper, a long note. Slipped inside was a faded yellowed photo of three Chinatown teenagers, a photo he hadn't seen in years but remembered well. *There were three of them then. Himself, Lucky, and Wing Lee. Now he was, once again, the sole survivor.*

On the back of the photo, a scribbled *Castle Keep, chimney sweep.*

He unfolded the note, was surprised to see it opened with his name.

Jacky boy,

If you get this il be dead. (but you know that, haha) Anyway we had good times as kids . . .

Lucky's grade-school penmanship and poor grammar reminded Jack of junior high school days.

Remember where we left Wing's chain? The gold chain? (yur cross to bear now ha) You should pay respects sometimes.

Jack remembered the rooftops.

Remember we used to piss on that old guinea's garden? Haha.

There was a gap with a small scrawled *fuck . . .*

Anyways, here's the book. Goin ta fuck the On Yee, some Wo. Ghosts too. Lotsa bad police too. Turn snitch and rat out evrybody. Haha Yu gonna make Captain!

Jack was stunned. Lucky must've been stone drunk juiced-out to have written the note.

Good luck with life

Lucky's last words.

He pocketed the note and photo.

The black booklet opened to a page listing names, some written in Chinese, along with dates and dollar amounts. More pages followed, the On Yee's accounting of who killed whom, when, and for how much.

The Chinese names were nicknames in most cases, and Lucky penned in their real names in several instances. He'd coded the addresses: mo66 was 66 Mott Street, ba10 was 10 Bayard, and so forth.

He'd listed sixty to seventy Chinatown businesses paying off protection on Ghost Legion turf, Mott, Bayard, and Mulberry Streets. *A million-dollar racket.*

There was a separate list of cops taking bribes, badge numbers, some single entries but a few repeat offenders. Notations for which precincts, the amounts each one got, and for what purpose. *They'd be coughing up every Cantonese lobster and Tsingtao beer they partied on without paying. Every Hamilton palmed for looking the other way.*

More bloody triad money fueling corruption, misery, and murder.

The list of dirty cops included:

PO Joe Ryan, Sgt. Nick Morillo—5th Pct.

PO James Song—1st Pct.

PO Richard Ramirez—9th Pct.

PO Andrew Lin—108th Pct.

Sgt. Akeem Jackson—7th Pct.

The list went on. *Civilian employees. Guards at the Tombs. Rikers Island custodians.*

He knew the book had incriminating information and could involve other ongoing investigations from different departments, like IAD, Internal Affairs. When the OCCB and FBI and Immigration got through with it, bad cops and bad people would fall hard.

Lucky had dealt him a winning card. He was going to play that card to help take down tongs and triads that leeched off the people of the neighborhood, the community he loved, the working folks Pa had always sided with.

He figured to get a promotion, a pay raise, maybe better assignments. Any IA crusade against him would be quashed, and Hogan and DiMizzio would hate him even more, if that was possible.

He also sensed the OCCB, and the FBI, could try to recruit him. *Political?*

He left the Mustang, hearing *remember the rooftops* in his head.

THE *high ground* was three blocks away, the rooftops on that stretch of Henry Street he hadn't visited in a dozen years. They were kids then and the rooftops held the hard secrets and memories of their youth.

What was once the gritty hardscrabble playground had been transformed. Garbage-strewn lots and fetid alleyways had given way to supermarkets, a new church, schools, and a community center. The outward progress reminded him how the Chinatown of his father had changed, but too late for him, the son.

Death and bloodshed had driven him out to Brooklyn.

He entered 29 Henry, went to the roof. The latch on the roof door was the same and he popped it easily.

On the roof, not much had changed, just the tar cover repatched in a few places. Everything else still a jumble of air ducts, skylights, and chimneys.

By memory he went left, crossing the building lines. There were no clotheslines out, but he had to squeeze past milk crates supporting someone's trays of home-salted butter fish.

Pay ya respects sometimes.

When he reached No. 37 he turned to the rear of the building. There was a chimney there, long since abandoned after the building had been renovated.

The flattop chimney had a wood board covering it, crudely sealed around the edges with a crusty stucco-like material. It looked like it hadn't been touched in years.

Remember where we hung Wing's chain?

Looking around, he found part of a metal antenna he could use to pry off the wood board. He was surprised to see how easily it lifted off. The seal was just *cosmetic*, to keep out little birds and critters probably.

He looked inside the hole, and where he might have seen Wing Lee's thin gold chain was a bag instead. A weather-worn old-style zippered gym bag, like school kids used to carry, crammed into the chimney hole.

He grabbed it with both hands and yanked it out.

Pay ya respects? Not bothering to dust it off, he took a *fighting* breath and unzipped it.

The first thing he saw was Wing's skinny gold chain,

carefully taped onto black plastic. The black plastic turned out to be a garbage bag.

He pulled the chain free and pocketed it. Took a *sustaining* breath as he spread the plastic.

The garbage bag was full of money. *Fat bundles of Jacksons and Grants.* Some of Lucky's *dailo* loot.

Glancing around to see no one had witnessed the discovery, he quickly estimated it was a twenty-thousand-dollar stash. He closed it up, zipped the gym bag, and double-checked the chimney again. *Empty.*

He headed back toward No. 29, imagining three Chinese American juveniles, their younger selves, wreaking mischief on the world below. *A brotherhood of Chinatown boys.* He was now the sole survivor once again, the last man standing.

What to do with all the money? Lucky sure didn't need it anymore. The money was way more than enough to cover potter's field.

By the time he bounced down onto Henry Street, he'd decided to call Vincent Chin and visit *The United National.*

It was time to call in a favor.

THE NEXT MORNING, he was buying incense at the Temple Store, along with a cardboard miniature of a red Mercedes coupe. No death money, no paper abalone, no offerings of ritual foods. *Keep it simple,* Lucky had always said.

Just enough to fill a one-foot-square hole in his heart.

He was paying the monk cashier when a call jangled his phone. *Alexandra calling.*

He was happy to hear her voice, all the tough and tender notes there, rather than clandestinely communicating through lifeless texts and shorthand messages.

They followed each other's sentences like there was a time limit on the conversation.

"I was awarded full custody," Alex said. "*He* got supervised visits."

"Good news," Jack said. He was happy about her long-awaited victory and didn't want to darken anything with news of Lucky's death.

"And I need to get Kimberly to understand the visitation arrangements. "

"These things take time," he said.

"And we're going to Hong Kong for three weeks. She'll meet her cousins for some bonding, before school starts."

He was quiet a moment, unhappy that Alex would be away for the near future.

"Have a *great* trip," he heard himself saying. "Going to miss you."

Awww. Going to miss you too. He liked the thought of it.

"By the way," she added. "Your friend from the newspaper came by with a donation."

"My *friend?*" he feigned surprise, still drinking in her voice.

"Vincent, the *manager*," she continued, "brought a red envelope."

"A *lai see?*"

"Lucky money. An anonymous check for eighteen thousand."

"That's a *sweet* lai see."

"Lucky for us, too. We just lost some state funding for the Women's Center."

"Anonymous."

"Yeah, still some good people out there." *Ironic*, thought Jack. He was glad Lucky's money would be put to good use.

"You sound tired," she noted.

"Yeah, been losing sleep."

"Cop stuff?"

"Yeah. But also thinking of *you.*" It wasn't a lie.

"*Awww*, we'll get together after Hong Kong, okay?"

"That's a bet then."

It was all he could hope for.

Ashes and Dust

IT WASN'T LIKE there was a funeral at the Wah Fook parlor. No one else came, as he'd expected, when they gave him the box of Lucky's ashes. He'd had to sign for it.

There were no twenty black cars in a funeral cortege, no overflowing flower wagon. There was no mournful Chinese dirge, no shiny brass casket shouldered out by weeping family.

There was just him taking out the ashes, headed for a hole in the ground.

He put the box of ashes in a bag with the incense and the little red cardboard Mercedes, let it ride the shotgun seat as he drove the Mustang out to Queens Calvary.

It was a sunny half-hour drive and he was parking in the cemetery lot when he caught the message. *From May McCann.*

Need to talk? You're not alone. Make appointment. I'm available.

For a moment it seemed like an ad from a porn site. But he couldn't help remembering her pretty face, that steel smile in her eyes. *Could she have seen his Tsun Jin report in his file already?*

You're not alone.

He never felt *more* alone, and wasn't sure how to explain it. His cop life intruding on his civilian life again. Not sure if he should keep a cap on his feelings, or those fleeting instants where his free soul didn't need to be a New York City cop anymore, didn't need to justify anything. Didn't need to serve or protect or *kowtow* to anyone.

The gravestones beckoned and he tabled her message for the time being.

Goodbye

POTTER'S FIELD WAS a patchy brown strip that followed the rear wall, the gritty highway side of the big cemetery.

Lucky's hole was tucked away in the far corner, past the hilly pastoral dead lands. Just where the Wah Fook drivers described—*the constant roar of the highway, the soot-spewing trucks*. A one-foot-square hole. Neat at the edges, the dug earth a small mound to its right. Big enough for a jade plant or a box of ashes and dressing. He imagined the spade booted in, churning up the earth, down its length a foot, *a couple of times front and back*.

Square it up.

The black marker was a brick-sized polished stone, *included* in the funerary deal, with the name TAT carved into its face. His *proper* name. Not Lucky.

Jack took a breath, emptied the plastic bag. *Keep it simple*. No firecrackers, the evil spirits already scared enough of Lucky anyway.

No food offering.

No death money.

No bowing.

He placed the box of ashes into the hole, took out his

lighter, and fired up three sticks of incense. Planting those by the polished brick stone, he torched the little red Mercedes.

"Here's a cool set of wheels, Tat," he said quietly. "Roll like *you know*." He held the burning little car until its flames singed his fingers, its glowing ashes following into the hole.

Live big or die small, Lucky's cheap advice.

He took out the pint of XO from Chinatown Liquors, Lucky's favorite jolt, poured a big wet circle around the hole.

Here's to you, kid.

Taking a long Buddha breath, he nudged the earthy mound back into the hole, covering up what remained of one of Chinatown's most feared *dailos*.

He tamped down the earth with his boot.

The world looked small, he thought, and drained the rest of the XO.

No one saw the tears in his eyes as he walked back to the lot.

There was still much to do, and the Mustang was waiting to take him back to Chinatown.

Acknowledgments

MUCH LOVE TO my longtime publisher, Soho Press, for the inclusiveness, to Bronwen Hruska my Boss Lady, to my keen no-nonsense editor Mark Doten, and to the hardest working Crew in the business—Paul Oliver and Juliet Grames, Meredith Barnes, Rudy Martinez, Amara Hoshijo, Abby Koski, Kevin Murphy, Rachel Kowal, Carin Siegfried, Daniel Ehrenhaft, Janine Agro—I luv you all!

A special bow to my Chinatown *hing yau*—brothers, sistas, friends—you amaze me all the time.

Great gratitude to my Agents—Dana Adkins and Debbie Phillips—for cheering me on, crunching the numbers, and always having my back.

Thanks also to my friends at Hamilton Madison House, Asian American Writers Workshop, the Organization of Chinese-Americans, the Museum of the Chinese in America (MOCA), the Mystery Writers of America, and Project Reach—*you know who you are*.

And humble love to Doris Chong always, to Geoff Lee, Shon Chen Tyler, Shemy Koo, Andrew Chang, and Nancy Chu.